Thomas Linn

The Health Resorts of Europe

a medical guide to the mineral springs, climatic, mountain, and seaside health

resorts, milk, whey, grape, earth, mud, sand and air cures of Europe

Thomas Linn

The Health Resorts of Europe
a medical guide to the mineral springs, climatic, mountain, and seaside health resorts, milk, whey, grape, earth, mud, sand and air cures of Europe

ISBN/EAN: 9783337287900

Printed in Europe, USA, Canada, Australia, Japan

Cover: Foto ©Andreas Hilbeck / pixelio.de

More available books at **www.hansebooks.com**

THE
HEALTH RESORTS OF EUROPE.

A MEDICAL GUIDE TO THE MINERAL SPRINGS, CLIMATIC, MOUNTAIN, AND SEASIDE HEALTH RESORTS, MILK, WHEY, GRAPE, EARTH, MUD, SAND, AND AIR CURES OF EUROPE.

BY

THOMAS LINN, M.D.

Doctor of Medicine, Faculty of Paris; Doctor of Medicine and Surgery, University of New York; Member of the British Medical Association; Member of the Continental Anglo-American Medical Society; Membre de la Société de Médicine Pratique de Paris; Membre de la Société de Médicine et Climatologie de Nice; Physician to the Bathing Establishments at Aix-les-Bains and Marlioz. In Winter at No. 16, Quai Masséna, Nice, France.

WITH A PREFACE

BY

A. E. SANSOM, M.D., F.R.C.P.

Physician to the London Hospital; Consulting Physician, North Eastern Hospital for Children; etc.

LONDON :

HENRY KIMPTON,
82, HIGH HOLBORN, W.C.

HIRSCHFELD BROS.,
BREAM'S BUILDINGS,
FETTER LANE, E.C.

1893

CONTENTS.

PREFACE.

I suppose it will be agreed that the majority of mankind can be divided into two classes—those who travel, and those who wish and hope to do so. The minority who revolve in a narrow orbit around their native place and have no desire to deviate into unexplored regions, is by no means considerable. The book of my friend, Dr. Linn, appeals to the majority, which may again be divided into a small group of doctors and a large group of patients and those in whom doctors are interested. It is probably because I have had an acquaintance, more or less intimate, for the space of half-a-century, with these various groups of humankind as well as with the places to which they tend in search of the treasures of health that I have been privileged to write these prefatory remarks. I shall use my privilege in the manner of a candid friend.

First, I shall address my advice to the largest group—to those who are most interested, who have not received a medical education, but want to know something about health resorts. Some of these, overworked in professions or businesses, for example, are not sufferers from definite diseases, but evince a most laudable desire for change of scene and air. It is not necessary for them to be steamed at Bouillon-les-Bains, fried at Sonnenschein-vor-der-Höhe, nor alternately warmed and cooled on the heights of Monte Excelsa, but their mental orchestrion wants to have the stop changed. The cells of a portion of their brain overworked, and accustomed to work in a certain way, long for a holiday, and are greatly relieved when a chance is given to other groups of cells which are elaborators of the intellect, the emotions or the will. In others, however, disease,—it may be the slight and gradual unfolding of the evil seed or the marked development of a distressing malady—compels the patient to think of the climatic treatment of symptoms that medicines are ineffectual to check. Let me counsel all these first to read this book, secondly, to take the advice which the author of this book gives, viz., to consult with their own doctors before determining where they shall go. It is probable, my esteemed friend, that your own doctor has more knowledge of the subject, and a more sincere desire for your welfare, than a perfect stranger has. If your valuable watch begins to go wrong, or if a flaw shows itself in an important piece of machinery, you take advice of a watchmaker in the one case, an educated engineer in the other. But is it not the case that when you contemplate a step that may materially influence your health and your prospects of longevity, you are rather inclined to chat the matter over with Mrs. Lively, the pale lady very admirably got up, who is always running about Europe enjoying herself? Or, perhaps, for the relief of your pains and aches, instead of following the advice of your doctor to adopt climatic treatment, you con-

sult the advertisement columns of a news-
paper, and spend a sum sufficient to procure
for you a nice little holiday in the purchase
of an uncomfortable Electro-galvano-Jupiter-
cum-Minervâ-fulgurific belt (constructed of
common flannel with little bits of iron wire
sewn therein), recommended by its vendor,
a self-dubbed professor, who has been, say,
a hitherto unsuccessful trader or an ex-assis-
tant in an old curiosity shop.

And now may I turn to offer, with all
respect, my candid advice to those of my
professional brethren who would send their
patients to European watering places?   First,
let me emphasise Dr. Linn's counsel that a
letter briefly embodying the doctor's experience of the patient's illness should be ad-
dressed to the professional brother practising
at the given health resort.   It is impossible
that a physician, living at a distance, shall
be sufficiently acquainted with the technical
methods of application of the local means of
cure, and with the modifications necessary at
the time of the patient's visit.   Balneological
and climatic methods of treatment are not

quite matters of sweet simplicity. From
some of the published books on Baths and
Waters, it would seem that the latter could be
prescribed readily and satisfactorily according
to their chemical characteristics. If that
were all, the reasoning would be very simple.
For example, this young lady, my patient,
is pale, anæmic. Her blood is deficient in
iron. I look up the list of watering-places
in which are springs containing iron in solution, and I send her to any one of those.
But why should she make a journey for this
object ? I could obtain a water for her to
drink, which should contain much the same
proportion of the desired medicament if I
left a few iron nails to rust in the pure element obtained at home. No, there is something more in the places indicated by Dr.
Linn than the facility for imbibing a fluid
which Mr. Samuel Weller described as having " a very strong flavour of warm flat-
irons." The pale and languid girl is taken
out of the narrow circle of home life to one
of the health resorts indicated in this book.
She breathes the pure air as well as swallow-

ing the iron-containing waters, and she con-
forms to the rules of early rising and judicious
regimen sanctioned by experience. Then
the dormant energy awakens, and the roses
return to the cheeks—not only because the
iron of the water has made its way into her
life-stream, but also because her lungs have
been filled with the pure air, and the great
arteries which go to the lungs and to the
system generally have become enlarged, so
that they distribute a larger, ampler current.

Or, to take another illustration, suppose
the patient to suffer some of the painful
symptoms in the heterogeneous group popu-
larly known as Rheumatism. The doctor
may see fit to send one of such patients to
Carlsbad, another to Vichy, a third to Aix-
les-Bains. All may improve and get well,
but the road to health in each case is a
different one. In the first, the imbibing of
the waters may produce a digestive crisis—
there may be a rather strong appeal to the
organs of elimination, and then a salutary
re-arrangement. In the second, a less pronounced but effectual change may be gra-

dually produced by the alkaline waters, systematically imbibed, upon the blood. In the third, the means of cure may make no direct appeal to the stomach, but there may be a re-adjustment of the relations between the skin and the internal organs by the judicious use of baths ; and the circulation may be aided by the system of massage carried out at Aix-les-Bains in the highest perfection. So the desired result is arrived at by varying modes. In the case of what is called Rheumatic Gout the lesson may be enforced even more strikingly. The case which rebelliously refuses to improve at one place will steadily tend towards recovery in another. This is not surprising to those who believe that the disease in question is not one in which a poison like that of rheumatism is circulating in the blood, nor one like gout, where crystalline salts are deposited around the joints, but one where the prime cause is in the nervous system which dominates all and disposes to the aberrant processes in the joints. Few will dispute that a great number are *mixed* cases in which the various factors operate in various degrees.

These are arguments which tend to show that there is only one reliable guide for the invalid who seeks for recovery at a health resort—that is, EXPERIENCE. *A priori* arguments are not entirely satisfactory. Most of the waters were discovered not by any process of subtle reasoning, but by a fortuitous concourse of circumstances. It is said that the hot springs of Bath were found by the leper Bladud, son of Hudibras, whose diseased pigs wallowed therein and were cured, their master following with success their example ; that those of Carlsbad were discovered by a stag running before Charles IV. and his companion hunters into the scalding water and giving evidence of its effects ; that the warm springs of St. Gervais were found by the shepherds whose goats delighted to plunge and frolic therein. At all the various resorts the perfecting of the arrangements, and the selection of suitable cases have been the work of many years—of centuries in some instances. So Science has fulfilled herself in many ways : and Science is but common sense perfected.

Let me commend these pages to all who seek by means of change of scene and climate to obtain restored health and renewed vigour, whether in places where Heaven's pure sun and air constitute the ways and means—or where baths, such as the Romans said made life worth living for, are the agencies for good—or where the Æsculapian Deity,

> " The streaming bowl
> Gives to his pale-eyed suppliants, wafts the seeds,
> Metallic and the elemental salts,
> Washed from the pregnant glebe."

Thus may Apollo again and again triumph over Python.

A. ERNEST SANSOM, M.D.

London, April, 1893.

AUTHOR'S PREFACE.

THE treatment of acute disease has been much improved in our time. But neither the materia medica nor the newer surgical operations have much value in the relief or cure of those constitutional states called chronic maladies; and for these some of the best forms of treatment are found in mineral waters, climatic resorts, sea-baths, and other hygienic therapeutical agents. It is quite possible that other waters are equal in medicinal value to those that are so much used in Europe, but it is certain that no other health resorts have reached the point of perfection that those abroad have. This is partly owing to the large experience gained by physicians who devote themselves to a life at these springs, and also to the fact that enterprising companies have built magnificent establishments there. Often it is the effect of climate, or the method of applying the waters, rather than their intrinsic value, that makes a cure. The years of accumulated evidence and experience, and the thousands of accurate medical observations that have been made of the effects of mineral waters and climate, will readily account for the preference given to the old European baths, springs, and mountain and seaside resorts.

We have endeavoured to make this Medical Guide to Europe as concise as possible ; finding that nowadays people will not read long treatises and writing for the general public, as well as for physicians, we have explained the technical terms used, so that they may be easily understood by all.

The usual guides are written by non-professional people, and while they give some correct information they contain errors that make them useless from a medical point of view. Others give long lists of insignificant places that are unfrequented by Anglo-American people, and that do not have the comforts and conveniences expected by English-speaking visitors.

We purpose, therefore, to describe very *briefly*, but give *all the necessary* information to the important medical stations in Europe, but not to pad the book with little known places. All the resorts are written up from a medical point of view, and special attention is paid to the sanitation of each station and to its general hygiene, as well as to the cure of disease by climate and mineral waters.

We have availed ourselves of the latest monographs and works on the question, as far as the medical portions are concerned. Local physicians have been asked to examine the accounts given of their stations; and when we add that we have personally visited and studied very many of the stations in Europe, besides having for a long time sent patients to be treated at many of them and observed the results, we trust that this will be taken as a guarantee of the correctness of the information given in the text.

No analyses are given of the various waters, as those made have considerable

B

discrepancies; and it is more than probable that the mineral constitution of the springs varies from time to time. Still more: the indications for treatment that are derived from the chemical composition of mineral waters are not the most important ones. An analysis, be it ever so correct, is seldom of much use to the patient, and it often conveys only the vague idea that should he drink such waters he would absorb a great number of complex chemical substances.

Much care has been given to the preparation of a list of all the English and American physicians and specialists who reside and practise in Europe. The shortest and best routes from London and Paris to the various localities named are given, with the distance and the first-class fares. Good hotels are recommended in each place.

This guide is strictly independent; no address given is paid for. Yearly new editions will be published and all changes noted.

This manual was written because no one book gave us the information we needed.

We hope it will be useful, both to the public and to those of our professional brethren who may not have had the opportunity of frequenting the European resorts and making personal observations there; and that it will increase the use and the appreciation of the means of healing that nature has so abundantly supplied.

THOMAS LINN, M.D.

Nice and Aix-les-Bains, France.

ABBREVIATIONS USED.

TABLES OF FOREIGN MONIES.

THERMOMETER AND WEIGHTS.

P.L.M.—Paris, Lyons and Mediterranean Railroad.* Station, Gare de Lyon.

S.F.R.R.—South of France Railroad. Station, Gare d'Orléans.

N.F.—North of France Railroad. Station, Gare du Nord.

E.F.—East of France R.R.W. Station, Gare de Strasbourg.

W.F.—West of France. Station, Gare St. Lazare.

Lat.—Latitude.

Long.—Longitude.

Alt.—Altitude.

Pop.—Population.

S.G.—Specific Gravity.

---

* Paris R.R. Stations are called Gare de ——

MONEY TABLE.

Approximate Equivalents.

American Money.		English Money.			French* Money.		German Money.		Austrian Money.	
Doll.	Cts.	L.	S.	D.	Fr.	Cent.	M.	Pf.	Fl.	Kr.
—	1	—	—	$\frac{1}{2}$	—	5	—	4	—	2
—	2½	—	—	1¼	—	12½	—	10	—	5
—	5	—	—	2½	—	25	—	20	—	10
—	10	—	—	5	—	50	—	40	—	20
—	12½	—	—	6¼	—	62½	—	50	—	25
—	20	—	—	9¾	1	—	—	80	—	40
—	25	—	1	—	1	25	1	—	—	50
—	50	—	2	—	2	50	2	—	1	—
—	75	—	3	—	3	75	3	—	1	50
1	—	—	4	—	5	—	4	—	2	—
1	25	—	5	—	6	25	5	—	2	50
1	50	—	6	—	7	50	6	—	3	—
1	75	—	7	—	8	75	7	—	3	50
2	—	—	8	—	10	—	8	—	4	—
2	25	—	9	—	11	25	9	—	4	50
2	50	—	10	—	12	50	10	—	5	—
3	—	—	12	—	15	—	12	—	6	—
4	—	—	16	—	20	—	16	—	8	—
5	—	1	—	—	25	—	20	—	10	—
25	—	5	—	—	125	—	100	—	50	—
125	—	25	—	—	625	—	500	—	250	—

* French, Italian and Swiss money are the same.

CENTIGRADE THERMOMETRIC SCALE TURNED INTO FAHRENHEIT.

C.	F.	C.	F.	C.	F.	C.	F.	C.	F.	C.	F.
100	212.0*	80	176.0	60	140.0	40	104.0	20	68.0	0	32.0†
99	210.2	79	174.2	59	138.2	39	102.2	19	66.2	— 1	30.2
98	208.4	78	172.4	58	136.4	38	100.4	18	64.4	— 2	28.4
97	206.6	77	170.6	57	134.6	37	98.6‡	17	62.6	— 3	26.6
96	204.8	76	168.8	56	132.8	36	96.8	16	60.8	— 4	24.8
95	203.0	75	167.0	55	131.0	35	95.0	15	59.0	— 5	23.0
94	201.2	74	165.2	54	129.2	34	93.2	14	57.2	— 6	21.2
93	199.4	73	163.4	53	127.4	33	91.4	13	55.4	— 7	19.4
92	197.6	72	161.6	52	125.6	32	89.6	12	53.6	— 8	17.6
91	195.8	71	159.8	51	123.8	31	87.8	11	51.8	— 9	15.8
90	194.0	70	158.0	50	122.0	30	86.0	10	50.0	—10	14.0
89	192.2	69	156.2	49	120.2	29	84.2	9	48.2	—11	12.2
88	190.4	68	154.4	48	118.4	28	82.4	8	46.4	—12	10.4
87	188.6	67	152.6	47	116.6	27	80.6	7	44.6	—13	8.6
86	186.8	66	150.8	46	114.8	26	78.8	6	42.8	—14	6.8
85	185.0	65	149.0	45	113.0	25	77.0	5	41.0	—15	5.0
84	183.2	64	147.2	44	111.2	24	75.2	4	39.2	—16	3.2
83	181.4	63	145.4	43	109.4	23	73.4	3	37.4	—17	1.4
82	179.6	62	143.6	42	107.6	22	71.6	2	35.6	—18 —	0.4
81	177.8	61	141.8	41	105.8	21	69.8	1	33.8	—19 —	2.2

The centigrade thermometer is used all over Europe. * 100 C. is 212 Fah., boiling point. † 0 C. is 32.0 Fah., freezing point. ‡ 37 C. is 98.6 Fah., man's normal temperature.

TABLE OF FOREIGN WEIGHTS AND MEASURES REDUCED INTO ENGLISH.

Kilos.				lbs.	ozs.	Kilos.				lbs.	ozs.
1	...	...	...	2	3	7	...	...	...	15	6 $\frac{9}{10}$
2	...	...	...	4	6	8	...	...	...	17	10 $\frac{1}{2}$
3	...	...	...	6	10	9	...	...	...	19	13 $\frac{1}{3}$
4	...	...	..	8	13	10	...	...	..	22	0 $\frac{1}{4}$
5	...	...	...	11	1 $\frac{1}{8}$	50	...	...	...	110	4
6	...	...	...	13	4	100	...	...	...	220	7

One Metre = 39.37,079 English Inches, or about 1 Yard and 3⅓ Inches.

One Kilometre = 1,093⅗ Yards = nearly ⅔ of a Mile.

One Litre = 0.2,200,968 Imperial Gallon, or nearly ¾ Pint.

The " Kilo " Weights are used in all Europe now.

HEALTH RESORTS OF EUROPE.

INTRODUCTORY HINTS AND ADVICE.

The Choice of a Watering-Place. — We suppose in the first instance that we are speaking to invalids going to some European watering-place, or intending to winter in one of the health resorts abroad. The first advice we give is to see a physician before doing so, and not to take counsel of some kind friend who may have been benefited by such and such waters, or by living in a certain climate. Very often he will not have an exact notion as to the precise place where the kind of treatment he proposes can best be carried out, nor have tried the watering-places there ; but he can always give the best advice as to the kind of water or climate,

1

and no person should come abroad without having competent professional advice, either from him, or from some specialist, with a written diagnosis or history of his case together with a probable prognosis.

When located, the invalid should not be travelling around to neighbouring places, but should give a fair and perfect trial to the climate or waters and situation so carefully selected by the home physician, with a direct view to his special benefit and improvement.

The place and country are also important, but once having decided the sort of treatment, it may be partly left to individual choice where it shall be carried out, and here our Guide will help. For instance, if iron waters are ordered, the patient can look over the list in each country, and decide for the one that suits him best. He can also inspect the therapeutical index for his malady, and see what places are mentioned that would be nearest to his line of route.

We must repeat that an invalid should not select his summer or winter resort without competent advice, or it may be detrimental to him. This haphazard, unscientific selection of mineral-spring waters for their curative effects is the cause of a vast amount of complication in diseases of a chronic nature.

Patients often go from one spring with the system saturated with sulphur, iron, magnesia, lithia, or other drugs, to other springs where additional agents are thrown in upon the human tissue through the drinking of waters of springs to which they should never resort. The method usually counteracts the benefit of the properly-selected remedy, which has been chosen for the case.

The Time to go.—Nearly all the summer bathing stations are crowded in July and August. Some English people prefer May, or even October; but the immense majority of people go to the resorts in summer time, and as a rule they are right in doing so. The greater number of invalids, rheumatic and others, require the direct heat of the sun as well as the waters, for fear of catching cold while undergoing the bath treatment; and most of these springs are in mountain regions where it is often quite cool, if not cold, in the morning and evening, even in summer, and much more so in May and October. On the other hand, economic reasons will make some patients prefer the early and late months. During the full season the hotels demand the highest prices for rooms, and the baths are filled to repletion, so that one cannot always carry out the treatment as one would wish. The baths themselves are given at a lower price before May 15th and after September 15th.

Preliminary Treatment.—Having decided on the time of starting, the question of treatment before going arises. In the old times no one went to a thermal or mineral water station without first going through a medicinal course of preparatory treatment. People are nowadays quite indifferent to this; but the omission is an error, and our readers should first consult their physician on this point before going to any mineral spring, or changing a climate.

Duration of Treatment. — Many of the mineral water-cures have fixed the duration of treatment quite arbitrarily at three weeks;

but this must largely depend on the patient and his malady. In reality every one requires a longer or a shorter time, depending on many conditions which the doctors at the stations are in the habit of watching for. It may, however, be remarked that at many strong mineral springs most people become saturated, as it were, with the mineral elements in from three to four weeks; and then it is wise to rest for a longer or shorter time before taking a new course of baths or waters. The results of mineral water cures very often do not show themselves for some time after the cure has been made, as the mineral elements continue to work in the system for a long time after taking them into the body. It must be admitted that it is very often necessary to take more than one summer's treatment at many of the health resorts. Indeed it is not reasonable to expect a complete cure of a chronic malady in one season, although it often happens. This is even more true of the climatic cures. No fallacy is more widely spread, and none is less based on reason and experience than the expectation of immediate or rapid cure from change of climate. Chronic maladies, ingrafted as it were on the system, can only gradually be transformed and safely cured. Every patient should have a suitable companion to accompany him or her during the treatment.

Winter Resorts.—It is quite useless for invalids to go to the winter stations, as the gay world does in December, and expect to derive benefit from the climate. If a tendency to a disease is to be checked, or a real complaint cured, the early cold days of the north are to be avoided. In northern Europe the rainy, cold time comes on, as a rule, soon after the twentieth of September. Then the winter is approaching for the invalid, and he should leave the north before catching the first cold, which does so much harm and is so hard to get rid of, even in the south, for the rest of the winter. We must also caution the invalid not to leave his winter station too early in the spring, as he will find great difficulty in passing safely through the rapid alternations of the spring months in the north. We therefore urge upon him the greatest care then, and in place of leaving in April, advise him to stay in the south until the middle or the end of May. While speaking of climate we may say that the climate which will allow the greatest amount of out-door exercise (passive or active), and constant exposure to the open air, is in general the best one for invalids of all kinds. Except to relieve symptoms, modern medicine has nothing to cure many chronic maladies that can in any way compare with out-door treatment, and the constant exposure to Nature's own great cure—the oxygen of pure air. It seems almost strange that we see before us constant examples of this in the ruddy faces of the coachmen and other out-door workers, and take no note of it. Often they are under bad conditions as to food and drink, and yet they are healthy. Even in country villages, which are often under very bad sanitary conditions, the purifying influence of the air gives a healthy colour to invalids who are constantly exposed to it; and much more so when the place itself has been selected expressly as a health resort. In the north confinement to the house is forced upon the invalid, and no matter how healthy the place may be, will result in bad effects on him; while the chance to get out and about in the open air will save the same person in the south. The nearest approach in Europe to an ideal climate where invalids can go out almost every day can be found in the French Riviera.

Money, Trains, Clothing.—Having arrived on the Continent, one is often astonished to find how much better known and respected the English gold sovereign is than other pieces. In any part of Europe it can be changed nearer to its value than any other money. It is, therefore, well to have a moderate supply of these useful tokens, as well as the usual letter of credit. We give the fares *from Paris and London* (1st class), and best and shortest routes, for the Channel viâ Dover mostly.

In France many of the best trains are first-class only, but still within a year past, owing to competition, many of the first-class expresses have some second-class wagons;

for instance, the night Italian express from Paris to Italy, Switzerland and Aix-les-Bains, second-class fare is one-third less, but very often no second-class carriages are put on the express trains. As a rule, we prefer night travelling for invalids. The trains are then of the best, many of them run sleepers, and it is best for a person in ill health to get over a journey than to ride all day, perhaps on the sunny side of a carriage, and arrive tired at night to stop over in a strange hotel. We have found from long experience that one is more tired out by stopping over one night on the road than by going through. This, of course, refers to stopping one or two nights on the road, and not to the plan of taking a short day-journey, and staying from three days to a week at each place. This delightful way of travelling is highly to be recommended.

It is well to take both summer and winter suits of ordinary clothing, as the climatic changes met with are often very sudden. But clothing is good and cheap on the Continent, and no difficulty will be found in getting any article needed. For underclothing the newer forms of net or open porous articles are excellent, yet we prefer the woollen, and other fabrics like it, to cotton.

Exercise Cure.—One of the forms of treatment regularly carried out in Germany, according to the instructions of Professor Oertel, is the so-called earth-cure, and English people are excusable for thus translating the phrase; but in reality it implies a mode of treatment by taking ascending walks. It may be objected that walking about for the sake of one's health is nothing new, which is true, or a part of the truth; but German physicians are clever in turning an old thing to new account, and patients, it must be admitted, take kindly to old things under fresh aspects. Tell an invalid to walk about, and he will not greatly value the advice; but prescribe the *exercise cure* or the method of Oertel, and he will do it. In a number of places the roads have been measured for this purpose, and the altitudes carefully marked, while coloured sign-boards put up indicate the height and distance that the physician orders in each case. It is certain that by a proper classification and regulation of exercise the weak will be prevented from doing more than is good for them, and indeed we all know that over-exercise does as much harm as none at all. Ascending walks to suitable elevations are certainly useful in heart disease, obesity and many other complaints. Arco, Meran and other German watering-places are making a speciality of this very rational cure.

Grape Cure.—Grapes have always been given by doctors to patients in fever cases, but only in recent times have they been used as a systematic cure. Their nutritive value is not great, although they contain a good deal of sugar. Grapes are often employed as a supplementary treatment after other cures, but it is more than probable that their curative value has been exaggerated. They are essentially a dietetic cure, and to be useful a moderate quantity only should be used. This treatment is given in dyspepsia, chronic constipation, gravel, chlorosis, intestinal catarrh, hæmorrhoids, &c. Montreux and Meran are the principal resorts.

Milk and Whey Cure.—-This was first used in Gais, in the Canton of Appenzell, Switzerland, about 1750. Milk is, of course, a complete food, the most nutritious supplied by nature, and especially when cooked nothing digests so well in a healthy stomach. Its good effects in all the kidney troubles are well-known. As to whey, it is generally laxative, and acts more distinctly than milk in this direction. It is also believed to increase the secretion of the mucous glands, the liver and the skin. The various applications of milk foods and cures are more expressly the physician's province, and cannot be entered into at length here. This cure can be carried out at home, or at any of the stations, and either independently or in connection with other treatment used at the place.

Arenation, or Sand and Earth Cures.— Covering the body with sand is a very old form of treatment. It is carried out at Arcachon, and at many other sea-side places in France and the rest of Europe. The patient is put into a hollow scooped out of the sand, and has a layer of damp, hot sand thrown over him while he is exposed to the sun. It causes free sudation, and stimulates the skin. The mud-bath is a variety of this treatment. The mud of rivers (Dax, France) and of hot springs in other places, is put into baths, and hot steam turned into it. The patient lies in the liquid mud, and after a certain number of minutes steps into a plain water bath, or is douched with clear water to take off the mud. The idea of these baths is that the mud contains the deposit of the waters, which ought to be the strongest part of the mineral constituents, and that they would constitute the best method for the use of the mineral for cure. We now know, however, that little, if any, of the principles enter by the skin, and it is probable that these cures act by the heat only. They are mostly used for chronic rheumatism, stiff joints and gout.

Medicines.—It is almost useless nowadays to carry drugs, as every little village has its chemist's shop where fresh medicine is dispensed. Still, some of the handy compressed tabloids now in use may be kept on hand, to be used with care in emergencies.

Beverages.—Ordinary drinking water, milk, and all non-alcoholic liquids should be boiled before using.   There is a prevalent but dangerous and quite unfounded idea that the impurities of such fluids can be corrected by mixing them with wine or spirits. This is entirely fallacious; they are not a whit less dangerous for being so mixed. The notion that a dash of brandy in water robs it of its unwholesomeness is a vulgar error that should at once be dismissed.   The artificial syphons of so-called seltzer water are most dangerous, being usually nothing more than any common water charged with carbonic acid gas.   It is wise not to drink any town water until one is sure of its quality, or gets accustomed to its use.   Plenty of good cheap mineral waters are to be had, bottled for drinking purposes, in Europe. In England, Apollinaris is used; in France, St. Galmier, Pougues, Vichy, Vals; in Germany and Austria ask for a bottle of Giesshübler.

While on the subject of bottled mineral waters, we must state that the assertion often made to the effect that their use will cure disease as well as treatment at the springs themselves, is absolutely untrue. A mineral water, be it ever so well corked and bottled, will be found perfectly good only for the first glass, and if the rest is kept, even for a day, it is practically useless in a medical sense. When a bottle of mineral water is opened, it should be all used as soon as possible.

At the Baths.—Do not drink more than the quantity of water ordered by the doctor, under the false idea that you cannot take too much of a good thing. Excess in this matter has been known to do great harm. Be careful to follow the alimentary regimen laid down, and on first coming to the country and the mountains do not attack the *table d'hôte* with your newly-found appetite. At many stations it is usual to take baths and waters at extremely early hours. This is by no means absolutely necessary. Indeed, many delicate people will do well to pass over this old-time custom, and drink and bathe as late as 10 a.m. So long as the waters are not taken too near a meal, either before or after it, there is no use in drinking them at unnecessarily early hours.

After Cures.—It is sometimes possible, in the case of the stronger waters, to continue their use at home after the regular cure. Certain of the stronger sulphur and arsenical waters, and the purgative ones, may be so used to advantage. In this case order *very small* bottles, and use them all when opened.

In other cases it is usual to take a course of alkaline or iron waters after sulphur ones, at the same place or elsewhere, or else to change mountain for seaside, or *vice versâ*, or again, to go home at once and rest. All these modifications of cures should be decided on by a physician. We need hardly say much on the danger of taking any mineral water without the advice of a doctor who lives and practises on the spot. The physicians of any particular place, be it a bath or a climatic station, have a knowledge of effects which are not apparent to the casual observer, and their daily experience is worth more than any knowledge gained from hearsay or even from books. We therefore cannot too strongly urge that patients should take advantage of the experience of a local doctor on going to any health resort.

Useful Articles to Carry.—A few words on this subject. The invalid should take along with him a spirit lamp to burn alcohol, as it is often difficult to get hot water, or to have any liquid boiled just when wanted. In all parts of Europe alcohol is sold cheap by the grocers for burning in these etnas or alcohol lamps. A flask of the best cognac should be carried, as this is a valuable medicinal agent, at least for those who are not unduly accustomed to its use. Next, a pocket-compass to get rooms that really face the sun south, or south-west,—*au midi*, as the French call it —for the obliging landlord will often declare that all his rooms face full south. A pair of smoked-glass spectacles is useful; so also are a thermometer, barometer and a rubber bag that will serve for hot water applications. It should have a large mouth, so

2

that it can be used for ice, to make cold applications, as well. Wax matches, pens, ink and soap must not be forgotten, not being supplied good abroad.

The Cost of Living Abroad, Fees, &c.— It is not an easy thing to give any accurate idea of what the cost of living may be at the watering-places. Fashion, the time of the season, the wants and the means of an invalid, and a thousand other factors have to be taken into account. In a general way, however, we may say that actual board and lodging will cost from ten francs (two dollars, or eight shillings) a head upwards. Many places are cheaper than this, but it would be unsafe to calculate on a less sum per day. When one settles down in an apartment, or in rooms with a kitchen, and has a little knowledge of the language of the country, the expense is much less, as food is not dear abroad, and rents are reasonable in comparison with other parts of the world. Physicians charge twenty francs (four dollars, or sixteen shillings) as a rule, for first consultations and visits ; the specialists, forty to sixty francs (eight to twelve dollars, thirty-two to forty-eight shillings). For instance, Professor Charcot and such men expect sixty francs at the office, and about one hundred for a visit. In England two guineas is a usual fee for consultations, and general practitioners take less for a continuous attendance. At baths it is usual to charge a certain sum for the season. An interesting table was lately drawn up showing the cost of living in different countries. Outside of the dear quarters in London, England would seem to be the most reasonable. Next comes Switzerland, 4 per cent. dearer; then Germany, 10 per cent. higher; then France, 15 per cent.; Italy, 20; and Pennsylvania, as representing the United States, 24 per cent. higher than England. This was determined by the expenditure on clothing, food, coal, gas and wages in each country.

CLASSIFICATION OF MINERAL WATERS.

WE make a very simple classification by grouping the waters under each country, according to the principal mineral element found in them. Patients ordered sulphur waters, for instance, will find all of those in Austria grouped together, all of those in France, &c.

The classes are—(1) sulphuretted; (2) saline; (3) purgative; (4) alkaline; (5) ferru-ginous. Seaside places are mentioned after these, then winter resorts. Grape, whey, sand, peat, mud, pine, hydropathic and electric baths are mentioned under each place having them.

1. *Sulphuretted or Sulphur Waters.*—In a general way these springs are exciting, and are best used by lymphatic persons whose skin is dry and hard. The triumph of the hot sulphur waters is in the treatment

of rheumatism, gun-shot wounds and joint-troubles; after these, in skin diseases, catarrhs of the bronchial tubes, chronic pleurisy and asthma. It must be understood that sulphur waters only succeed when these troubles are chronic. They are not used when there is any acute inflammation.

2. *Saline Waters.*—The pure salt waters are much used for scrofula, certain skin diseases, and bone and joint troubles. The purgative ones are, of course, useful in constipation, and in liver, spleen and abdominal diseases.

4. *Alkaline Waters.*—These have an extensive usefulness. The soda springs are of great importance in stomach troubles, by acting directly on the acid secretions of the body. They are most useful, therefore, in chronic maladies that have their seat in the viscera, liver, spleen, stomach, kidneys, &c.

5. *Ferruginous Waters.*—The iron waters are not so much made use of as they deserve, many physicians giving the drug directly. Anæmia and chlorosis are the principal indications, but not by any means

the only ones.   It should be mentioned that many of the other classes of waters contain iron, and that many of the alkaline group have arsenic in them.

THERAPEUTICAL INDEX AND DICTIONARY.

A FULL alphabetical list of diseases is given with indications of a suitable place for the treatment of each one, and an explanation or dictionary of the terms used. This list being made for the use of the general public as well as of physicians, we have thought it best to give the common names for all the diseases, and at the same time to explain the medical terms used.

Our object in making this therapeutical index is to indicate the places that are best suited to every malady, and while the exact indications for each mineral spring are much controverted, and form a difficult and delicate study, we are able to give the usual considerations from which a physician or a patient can choose a station suitable to the malady. Any disease not mentioned in this index is not amenable to treatment at health resorts.

Note.—*See the general alphabetical index for the number and page of the health resort mentioned and wanted.*

Abscess (a collection of pus or purulent matter).—See Boils, Tuberculosis.

Acidity.—See Dyspepsia.

Acne.—See Skin Diseases.

Adenitis (glandular inflammation).—Saline waters.   Uriage ; Baden-Baden ; sea baths. See Tuberculosis.

Addison's Disease (bronze-skin disease).— Vichy.

Ague.—La   Bourboule,   Royat,   Vichy, Bath, Tarasp, Carlsbad, Marienbad.

Albuminuria (presence of albumen in the urine). — Vichy, Vals, Carlsbad, Evian, Royat (if anæmia be present try the iron waters, also any pure spring water in large quantity), Schwalbach, Spa, Bath, Neuenahr, San Remo, Nice, Tunbridge Wells.

Alcoholism.—Vichy.

Alopecia.—See Baldness.

Amaurosis (obscurity of vision).—Brides,

Marienbad, Kissingen, Carlsbad, Voslau grape cure.

Amenorrhœa (stoppage of menses).—Aix-les-Bains, Baden-Baden, Schwalbach, Vittel, Franzensbad, Homburg, Bath, Néris, Kissingen, Kreuznach, Bushey, Pyrmont, Chianciano. For climate, the south — Nice, Cannes, Mentone.

Anæmia (deficiency of good blood).— Bagnères de Bigorre, Spa, Orezza, Schwalbach, Pyrmont, Forges, Levico, La Bourboule, Royat, St. Moritz, Bussang, Droitwich, Nauheim, Ems, Franzensbad, Tunbridge Wells, Levico, Amphion. Sea baths— Arcachon, &c. Climate cures — Egypt, Nice, San Remo. High Alpine resorts— Méran.

Anchylosis (fixed joints).—Dax, Aix-les-Bains, Bath, Malvern, Teplitz, Loëche, Baden in Switzerland, Acqui, Wildbad, Plombières.

Anthrax.—See Carbuncle.

Anorexia (want of appetite). --- High mountain resorts and seaside. See also Dyspepsia.

Angina.—See Throat Diseases.

Aphonia (loss of voice). — The sulphur waters. See Throat Diseases.

Aphthæ (thrush). — Vichy, and alkaline waters in general.

Arthritis.—See Rheumatism.

Ascites (dropsy). — Mineral waters are contra-indicated, but the warm climatic places may be useful—Egypt, Mentone.

Asthma.—Mont-Dore, Meran, St. Moritz, Scarborough, Malvern, La Bourboule, Schinznach, Allevard, Royat, Saint-Honoré, Enghien, Brighton, Bournemouth, Ems, Egypt, Nice-Cimiez, San Remo, Isle of Wight, Montreux.

Ataxy (*Locomotor*), (loss of power over the voluntary movements). — Uriage, Aix-la-Chapelle, La Malou, Aix-les-Bains, Gastein, Salins, Bushey, Bath. For the winter— Nice, Cannes, Nervi, San Remo.

Atrophy (muscular wasting).—Schwalbach, Baden-Baden, Aix-les-Bains, Dax, Salies de Béarn, Bath, Louèche.

Barber's Itch.—See Skin Diseases, under Tinea Sycosis.

Bile and Biliousness.—Vichy, Carlsbad, Cheltenham, Harrogate, Homburg, Marienbad, Tarasp.

Bladder, Diseases of—

,,   *Catarrh of.*—Contrexéville, Vittel, Evian, Pougues, Brides, Tarasp.

,,   *Cystitis.*—Vichy, Bath, Neuenahr, Alhama de Granada.

,,   *Incontinence of Urine.*—Néris, Saint-Sauveur, Plombières.

    Climates — Egypt, Mentone, Nice.

Blood (Determination of, to head).—Carlsbad purgative waters.

Boils and Carbuncles (Disposition to).—La Bourboule, Aix-les-Bains, Uriage, Schinznach, Carlsbad, Bagnères de Bigorre, Mont-Dore.

Breath (offensive).—See Dyspepsia.

Bright's Disease.—See Albuminuria. Malvern, Droitwich.

Bronchitis (chronic).—Ems, Cauterets, Challes, La Bourboule, Eaux Bonnes, Luchon, Saint-Honoré, Allevard, Royat, Mont-Dore,

Marlioz, Schinznach, Ischl. Whey cures. Climatic Treatment (when there is much discharge), Nice, Cannes, Mentone ; (for the dry form), Algiers, Pau, Bournemouth, Madeira, Meran, Montreux, Torquay.

Burns.—Vichy, and the alkaline waters.

Calculi (stone), *Biliary.*—Vichy, Pougues, Marienbad, Carlsbad, Vittel, Contrexéville, Ems, Montecatini, Castellamare.

  ,, *Urinary or Vesical.*—Vittel, Royat, Contrexéville, La Poretta, Evian, Franzensbad, Carlsbad.

  ,, *Uterine.*—See Uterus, diseases of.

Cancer.—For cancer of the womb and stomach hot waters are indicated, if only for relief of pain. The sulphur sources are too exciting, but cases may be sent to the hot alkaline springs : Vichy, &c.

Carbuncle.—See Boils. .

Caries (decay of bones).—Saline springs.

Catarrh (chronic forms only) :—

  ,, *Intestinal.*—Bath, Brides, Cheltenham, Homburg, Marienbad.

  ,, *Of nose.*—See Rhinitis. Ems Allevard.

Catarrh, Urethral.—The alkaline waters; Vichy, Pougues, Ems, Kreuznach.

„ *Uterine.*—See Uterus, diseases of. Ems.

„ *Pulmonary.*—Eaux Bonnes, Cauterets, Marlioz, Ems, Royat, La Bourboule, Meran, Mentone, Nice, San Remo, Hyères.

Cerebral System (brain troubles).—La Malou, Balaruc, Carlsbad.

Chlorosis (Deficiency of the corpuscular elements of the blood), called Green Sickness. — Spa, Royat, Plombières, Pyrmont, Meran, Saint-Moritz, Clifton, Malvern, Homburg.

Chorea (St. Vitus's Dance).—Aix-les-Bains, Baden-Baden, Plombières.

Colic (Hepatic).—Vichy, Brides-les-Bains, Cheltenham, Harrogate, Marienbad, Carlsbad.

Constipation (or costiveness).—Carlsbad, Châtel Guyon, Brides, Montmirail, Cheltenham, Homburg, Kissingen, Leamington.

Consumption.—See Phthisis.

Congestion of Head.—Purgative waters.

Contraction of Muscles and Tendons.—
Sulphur waters, Aix-les-Bains ; and massage,
Malvern.

Confinement (when difficult).—Any warm
baths, and life in a warm climate during the
labour will make it much easier than in the
north.

Convulsions.—See Chorea.

Cough.—See Bronchitis.

Cystitis (inflammation of bladder).—See
Bladder, diseases of.

Convalescence.—Mountain   and   seaside
places and iron waters.

Debility.—Iron waters : Gastein, the Riviera
climate.

Diabetes (excessive flow of urine containing sugar).—La Bourboule, Vichy, Carlsbad,
Neuenahr, Clifton, Teplitz, Pougues, Tunbridge Wells, Vittel, Brides-les-Bains, Droitwich.

Dropsy (accumulation of fluid).—Carlsbad,
Cheltenham, Brides, Harrogate, La Bourboule, Aix-les-Bains, Baden-Baden, Bagnères
de Bigorre, Cauterets.

Dysentery.—Carlsbad, Montecatini, Spa.

Dysmenorrhœa (difficult and painful menstruation).—Uriage, Baden, Bath, Franzensbad, Alhama, Plombières. Climate.—Nice and the south in general. Menstrual cases do best in warm climates.

Dyspepsia (*acid form*).—Vichy, Neuenahr, Vals.

„ *Atonic.*—Pougues, Saint-Moritz, Spa, Brides-les-Bains.

„ *Painful.*—Plombières, Evian, Pougues.

„ *Flatulent.*—Saint-Sauveur, Niederbronn, Homburg.

„ *Catarrhal.*—Carlsbad, Marienbad, Brides, Châtel Guyon.

Dysuria (painful urination).—Vittel, Contrexéville.

Ear Diseases (chronic form).—Brides.

Eczema.—See Skin Diseases. Harrogate, Aix-les-Bains, Moffätt.

Emphysema (distension, with gas, of tissues).—Mountain climates ; Meran, Madeira, San Remo, Hyères, Costebelle.

Erysipelas.—Some chronic forms do well at sulphur baths.

Erythema (inflammation of skin).—Alkaline springs.

Eye Diseases.—These are very little aided by mineral waters. The warm climates are useful.

Flatulence.—See Dyspepsia.

Fractures (old chronic ones).—Baden, Dax, Teplitz, mud baths, salt springs, Acirale, Acqui.

Gall Stones.—See Colic (hepatic).

Gastralgia.—See Dyspepsia (painful).

Gastric Catarrh.—See Stomach, diseases of.

Gastric Ulcer.—Ditto.

Glands.—See Adenitis, Tuberculosis and Scrofula. Salins, Cauterets.

Gleet.—Contrexéville, Vittel, Pougues.

Gout.—Vichy, Royat, Dax, Wiesbaden, Teplitz, Evian, Marienbad, Homburg, Montecatini, Louèche, Uriage, Bath, Malvern, Aix-les-Bains.

Gravel (deposit in urine).—Contrexéville, Marienbad, Vichy, Pougues, Royat, and most alkaline waters.

Hæmatemesis (vomiting of blood from the stomach).—Vichy, Homburg.

Hæmaturia (blood from the bladder or urine.)—Spa, Carlsbad, Contrexéville.

Hæmoptysis (blood spitting from lungs).—See Phthisis.

Hæmorrhoids (piles).—Carlsbad, Franzensbad, Brides, Montecatini, Vittel, Homburg, Kissingen, Aix, Moffat, Strathpeffer.

Hay Fever.—Mountain places.

Headache.—Marienbad and purgative waters.

Hoarseness.—See Larynx, diseases of.

Herpes.—See Skin diseases. Aix-les-Bains, La Bourboule, Saint-Honoré, Cheltenham, Salins.

Hysteria.—Carlsbad, Franzensbad, Gastein, Spa, Bagnères de Bigorre, Lucca, Saint-Sauveur. For climate : Nice, Matlock.

Hypochondria.—Gastein, Nice, Saint-Sauveur, Matlock, Amphion, the Riviera, Nervi, San Remo, Néris.

Heart (Diseases of).—Arco, Meran, Spa, Pau, and warm climates—Nice, &c.

Hepatic Diseases.—See Liver, diseases of. Vichy, Carlsbad.

Heartburn.—See Acid Dyspepsia. Vichy.

3

Incontinence of Urine.—See Bladder, diseases of. Vittel, Contrexéville,

Intermittent Fever (after attacks of).—La Bourboule, Montmirail.

Impotence.—Châtel-Guyon, Franzensbad, Aix-les-Bains ; warm climates, sea baths.

Insomnia.—Mountain climates. Franzensbad, Marienbad, Wildbad.

Intestinal Catarrh.—Cauterets, Plombières, Carlsbad, Bagnères, Leamington.

Intestines (atony of). Carlsbad ; purgative waters.

Intestinal Obstruction.—Marienbad ; purgative waters.

Joints (diseases of).—Teplitz, Dax ; mud and sand baths.

Jaundice.—See Liver, diseases of. Carlsbad, Montecatini, Bath, Cheltenham.

Kidneys (diseases of).—Milk and whey cures, grape cures.

    ,,   *Chronic Nephritis.*—After all inflammation has gone send to Contrexéville, Vittel, Vichy, Royat, Evian, Matlock, Tarasp.

Larynx (diseases of).—Eaux Bonnes,

Clifton, Aix-les-Bains, Marlioz, Royat, Saint-Moritz, Maloya, Davos.

Leucorrhœa (whites).—Baden near Vienna, Bagnères de Bigorre, Spa, Franzensbad, Plombières, Ischl ; sea baths.

Lead Poisoning.—Ofen or Buda-Pesth.

Liver (diseases of).—Carlsbad, Vichy, Brides, Montecatini, Teplitz, Pougues, Clifton, Panticosa, Royat, Malvern, Leamington, Harrogate, Cheltenham.

Lumbago.—All hot springs.

Lymphatism.—See Scrofula. Salins, Cheltenham ; sea baths.

Lungs.—See Phthisis.

Lupus.—See Phthisis. Ofen or Buda-Pesth.

Malaria.—La Bourboule, Levico, Brides.

Morphinism.—Climate : Nice.

Myalgia (pain in muscles).—Aix-les-Bains.

Nephritis.—See Kidneys, diseases of.

Nervous Debility, Neurosis, &c. — Iron waters ; Gastein, Meran, Néris, Lucca, Bath, Ischl, Malvern, Schwalbach, Spa, Teplitz.

Neuralgia.—Néris, Plombières, Ischl, Gastein, Bagnères de Bigorre, St. Sauveur, Ems, Droitwich, Baden near Vienna, Spa, St. Moritz.

Night Sweats.—See Phthisis.

Nose (diseases of).—See Rhinitis.

Obesity.—Aix-les-Bains, Brides, Marienbad, Châtel-Guyon, Homburg, Meran (grape cure), Kissingen, Arco ; mountain walks.

Ozæna.—See Rhinitis.   Uriage.

Otorrhœa.—See Ear, diseases of.   Uriage.

Ovarian Troubles.—See Uterus.

Paralysis, Cerebral Form.—Balaruc, Gastein, Niederbronn, Malvern, Acqui.

,,   *Spinal   Form.* — Wiesbaden, Schinznach, Gastein, Mont-Dore, Néris, Plombières.

,,   *Rheumatic.* — Aix-les-Bains, Néris, Acqui, Valdieri, Harrogate, Bath, Baden-Baden.

,,   *Lead   Form.*—Cauterets, Luchon, Aix-la-Chapelle, Uriage, Ofen, Dax.

,,   *Senile.*—Balaruc.

,,   *Hysteric.*—Ems, Plombières.

,,   *Infantile*—Bourbon.

,,   *Syphilitic.*—See Syphilis.

,,   Climatic   treatment :   Nice, Cannes, Egypt, Mentone, &c.

Paraplegia. — Aix-les-Bains,   Lamalou,
Plombières, Gastein.

Phthisis (Consumption).— See also Tuberculosis.

„   *Torpid Form.* — Eaux Bonnes,
Mont-Dore, Meran, Cauterets,
Görbersdorf, Falkenstein, Ems,
Aix-les-Bains, Revard, Ischl,
Ventnor.

„   *Scrofulous Form.*—La Bourboule,
Torquay.

„   *Gouty or Rheumatic Form.*—Ems,
Royat.

„   Climates: Mentone, Davos-Platz,
Malaga, Madeira, Algiers.

Pott's Disease.—Salt Springs ; Salins, Meran.

Palpitation.—See Stomach, diseases of.

Pharyngitis.—See Throat, diseases of.

Pleurisy (chronic form). --- Saint-Honoré,
Algiers, Pau, Hyères, Mont-Dore.

Pleurodynia.—Aix-les-Bains, Meran.

Prurigo.—See Skin Diseases.

Psoriasis.--See Skin Diseases.

Pneumonia.—After treatment : Pau, Mentone, Nice.

Rheumatism (simple chronic form).—Aix-les-Bains, Bath, Buxton, Droitwich, Acqui, Nauheim, Baden near Vienna, Teplitz, Cauterets, Woodhall Spa, Malvern, Plombières.

,,   *With Nervous Diseases.*—Néris, Saint-Sauveur, Plombières, Matlock, Bath.

,,   *With Gout.*—Royat, La Bourboule, Pougues.

,,   *With Gravel.*—Vichy, Vittel, Carlsbad, Wiesbaden.

,,   *With Bronchial Catarrh.*—Mont-Dore.

,,   *With Skin Disease.*—La Bourboule.

,,   *With Syphilis.*—Aix-la-Chapelle, Aix-les-Bains.

,,   *With Deformed or Fixed Joints.*—Dax; Mud baths.

,,   Climatic treatment. — Nice, Mentone, the South, Egypt, Hyères.

Rickets.—See Scrofula. Uriage.

Rhinitis (chronic nasal catarrh).—Cauterets, La Bourboule, Mont-Dore, Royat, Luchon, Ems, Allevard.

NOTE.—The sulphur waters are best in passive, depressed subjects; excitable and nervous patients do best at alkaline springs.

Climatic treatment is effective; dry-air places, like Nice, Cannes, Egypt, cure these cases in two or three seasons.

Sciatica.— Aix-les-Bains, Bath, Buxton, Teplitz, Saint-Sauveur, Woodhall Spa.

Scrofula : first period, in children 2 to 10.—Seaside resorts and baths; Arcachon, Biarritz, Mentone, Nice, Cannes, Berck-sur-mer, Soden, Uriage.

,, Second period, adolescents 10 to 20.—Salt springs, Salies, La Bourboule, Ischl, Nauheim, Valdieri, La Paretta, Ledesma, Uriage.

,, Third period, adults.— Luchon, Aix-les-Bains, Baden, Eaux Bonnes, Saint Honoré, Enghien, Acqui, Malvern, Cauterets.

Spinal Disease.—La Malou, salt baths; Nauheim.

Sprain.—Aix-les-Bains, and hot sulphur waters.

Spermatorrhœa.—Gastein, Cauterets.

Sterility.—A number of baths claim (doubtfully) to cure it ; Franzensbad, Ems, Pougues, Marienbad, Schwalbach, Aix.

Syphilis.—Aix-la-Chapelle, Aix-les-Bains, Uriage, Archena, Harrogate ; but regular constitutional treatment must not be dispensed with.

Stomach, Diseases of.—Vichy and any gaseous alkalines ; Homburg.

,, *Atony of.*—Grape cure ; Voslau, Kissingen.

,, *Gastralgia.*—Plombières, Royat, Evian, Homburg.

,, *Dilatation.*—Carlsbad, Aix-les-Bains, Chatel-Guyon.

,, *Catarrh.*—Carlsbad.

,, *Ulcers.*—Vichy.

Skin Diseases: Acne.—Luchon, Aix-les-Bains, Ems, Schlangenbad, Schinznach.

Skin Diseases : Eczema.—Creuznach, Sal-
    ins, Aix-les-Bains, Levico.

,,   *Lichen.*—Ems, Franzens-
    bad, Levico, Schinznach.

,,   *Lupus.*—Ofen or Buda-
    Pesth.

,,   *Psoriasis.*—Levico, Nau-
    heim.

,,   *Pemphigus.* — Aix-la-Cha-
    pelle.

,,   *Prurigo.*—Néris, Luxeuil.

,,   *Tinea Sycosis.*—Sea-baths.

,,   *Urticaria.* —Franzensbad,
    Moffatt, Vichy.

Tuberculosis.—This term is used nowadays very often for Consumption, as well as the local troubles formerly called Scrofula, cold abscess, and rickets.

Tubercular children are treated with success at sea baths—Royat, Arcachon, Biarritz, Ostend, Scheveningen, Berck-sur-mer.

Very delicate and weak children had best be sent to the baths on the Mediterranean coast. This sea is very salt, has no breakers, and is in a warm climate. Cannes, Mentone,

Nice. Salt springs : Salies de Béarn, Nauheim. Sulphur waters : Cauterets, Luchon,
Challes, Marlioz, Baden near Vienna. Arsenical : La Bourboule, Royat, Saint-Honoré,
Teplitz.

Throat, Diseases of : Tonsillitis.—Aix-les-
Bains, Challes, Marlioz, Cau-
terets, Allevard.

,,   *Pharyngitis.* — Saint   Honoré,
Pierrefonds,   Enghien,   Soden,
Ems.

Ulcers.—Aix-les-Bains, Valdieri, Baden,
Uriage.

Uterus, Diseases of :

,,   *Catarrh.*—Baden   near   Vienna,
Franzensbad,   Saint   Sauveur,
Marlioz,   Luchon,   Pyrmont,
Schwalbach, Wiesbaden.

,,   *Tumours.*—Kreuznach.   Climate :
the Riviera.

Venereal Excess.—Gastein.

Varicose Veins.—Alkaline waters.

Worms.—Purgative waters.

Wounds.—Dax,   Aix-les-Bains,   Teplitz,
Barèges, La Bourboule.

DESCRIPTION
OF HEALTH RESORTS AND CITIES BY COUNTRIES.

———

AUSTRIA-HUNGARY.

IN the southern part of this empire the winters are short and mild, while snow is not often seen, but the summers are long and hot, so that it cannot be counted as a health-resort. The latitude is between 45° and 51° north. In the north the winters are long and cold, and the summers short and warm. The mean annual temperature of this district, which is the only one interesting to the health seeker, is about 48°; in Vienna it is 50°. In the mountains it varies from 37° to 41°. Hungary itself has a fine, bracing, cold climate, but it is almost entirely neglected by Anglo-American people. The waters called *Pullna* and *Sedlitz* are Bohemian springs, but the places themselves are not frequented, and no bath establishments exist. This is true of quite a large number of the well-known marks of table and purgative waters, as they are only used at home and bottled like the well-known *Hunyadi Janos* and others.

SULPHUR WATERS.

Baden, Austria, called *Baden-bei-Wien.* It is the ancient " *Thermæ Cetiæ.*"

Route. — Eight hundred-and-eighty miles from Paris, E. of F.R.R., viâ Strasburg and Munich, to Vienna, twenty-six hours. Frs. 134. From London, £8 12s. 6d. Baden is seventeen miles from Vienna by rail; half an hour by express trains.

Waters.—There are thirteen hot sulphur springs at 80° to 95° Fah., containing a clear water with much common salt and sulphuretted hydrogen in it. The waters have the well-known "bad-egg odour," and deposit a yellow crystalline substance, called Baden salts. They are laxative, diuretic and exciting.

Therapeutics. — The diseases that are mostly treated here are chronic rheumatism, gout, tuberculosis, scrofula, paralysis, bronchial catarrhs, leucorrhœa and other women's diseases ; also skin diseases.

Baden is a fashionable resort for the rich Vienna people. It is well-situated in a beautifully wooded mountainous district, and all the arrangements are on a magnificent scale. The altitude is 700 feet; the mean temperature, 50° Fah. ; population, 5,000 ; number of summer visitors, 18,000. The waters are said to resemble those of Aix-la-Chapelle, and the place itself, Baden-Baden. It is not so cold here as in Vienna in winter, so that the baths are kept open all the year ; but of course the summer season is the crowded one. As in most German places, there is abundance of good music in a fine *Kurhaus*. The town is healthy, and receives an abundant supply of water from the famous Vienna *Hochquellen* works.

For travellers who make Vienna their headquarters, and need a sulphur cure, the place is to be recommended. The treatment can be taken in the hotels, some sixteen of which are bath houses as well. There are also the well-known swimming baths, one of which will hold some 150 people, and where the ladies and gentlemen bathe together for hours at a time The bath is surrounded by balconies, from which the friends of the bathers can see and talk to them during the bath—a very sociable sight.   The earth-cure and whey-cure are given here.   The place is so convenient to Vienna that people often go into town to the early evening performances given at the theatres there, and return to Baden the same evening.

Promenades. — The park or Theresiengarten, Calvarienberg and Weilberg are interesting, also Burgeneck ruins, &c.

Physicians.—Drs. Barth and Schwartz.

Hotels.—City of Vienna, Munsch, Green Tree, Schwartz Adler, Hirsch, Löwe.

BAD-VÖSLAU.

This is a small place three miles from Baden, celebrated both for its vintages, and as a grape-cure.   It also has a weak ferruginous or indifferent mineral water spring. The town stands among pine woods on the top of a hill, and is much frequented by the Viennese.

Physicians.—Drs. Krischke, Verminger.

OFEN, OR BUDA-PESTH, HUNGARY.

Route.—1,037 miles from Paris, E. of F.R.R., viâ Vienna, thirty hours; 200 francs. From London, £11 1s.

Waters.—There are many mineral springs in and around Buda-Pesth. Four bathing establishments are to be found in Buda, and two outside. The Elizabeth baths are out in the suburbs, nearly five miles by omnibus. This spring is rich in sulphates, and is much frequented. The Margarethenbad is on Margarethen Island, above the city; it has a fine bathing establishment. Near Buda is a group of buildings over the well-known Hunyadi Janos spring, where the water is bottled and sent all over the world; but it is not drunk at the place.

Therapeutics.—Much the same as all the sulphur waters. Lupus and lead-poisoning may be mentioned as well.

Ofen or Buda.—This is a city with a population of over 66,000, opposite Pesth, on the Danube. Its altitude is 450 feet. The climate is rather cold and severe, with considerable wind. It is frequented by a large number of local visitors, but not by many English or Americans.

Physicians.—Von Heinrich, Verzar.

Hotels.—Stadt Debreczin, Sechenyi.

SALINE WATERS.

Ischl.

Route.—1,048 miles from Paris, E. of F.R.R., viâ Vienna, forty-three hours; 172 francs. £9 9s. from London.

Waters.—Ischl is a type of chloride of sodium waters in Austria. It has been known as such since the twelfth century. There are two springs, the water having a specific gravity of 1.200. The salt mine is three miles from the town, and supplies the brine for the baths and the mud-slime used. The water is laxative, but at the same time tonic. It is mostly used in baths.

Therapeutics.—The waters are used for scrofula-tuberculosis, as well as arthritic complaints, neuralgia and women's diseases; but many people come to Ischl for the mountain-air cure, as well as milk cures.

The altitude here is 1,535 feet, the population 6,000. The place is beautifully situated in the Salzkammergut of Traun, halfway between the fine lakes of Hallstadt and Traun. There are nearly 6,000 visitors, and the town is fashionable and expensive in July and August, when it is filled by the wealthy Viennese. The climate is an Alpine one and healthy, but rather warm in summer; at the same time it is soothing, equable and suited to nervous cases. Pine baths are given here. One may meet an emperor in its streets, as the place is a frequent resort of sovereigns. There is a fine *Kurhaus* and the promenades in the glorious scenery of Austrian Tyrol are magnificent.

Physicians.—There are twelve resident: Drs. Kahn, Fürstenberg, Steiger.

Hotels.—Victoria, Post, Bauer (on the hill outside the village) and the Kaiserin Elizabet.

PURGATIVE WATERS.

Carlsbad.

Route.—820 miles from Paris, viâ Strasburg and Eger, thirty hours; 140 francs. From London £5 8s. 9d. Twelve hours from Berlin or Vienna, eight from Dresden or Munich, five from Prague.

Waters. — These celebrated hot mineral springs are sixteen in number, eleven of which are prescribed by the doctors. They are bi-carbonated chloro-sulphated waters, and we class them for convenience as purgative ; but their curative effects do not depend only on purgation. They are largely used for drinking purposes, but baths of the waters and mud and douches of all kinds are given. The specific gravity of the Sprudel is given as 1.00503, and its temperature is 166°. The taste somewhat resembles that of very salt chicken soup, but the water is clear in colour.

The action of these waters varies according to the spring. In small doses they often produce constipation ; in large quantity they purge. They are considered purgative, diuretic and resolvent.

Therapeutics. — Catarrh of the stomach, bowels and bladder ; biliary and urinary calculi ; disorders of the liver, gout, rheumatism, diabetes, uterine diseases, hæmorrhoids, hysteria, dysentery. (Dr. London.)

Contra-indications. They should not be used in debility, or when renal complications are present.

Carlsbad, or Charles's Bath, sometimes written Karlsbad, and the most renowned of the German waters, is in Bohemia, 1,120 feet above the sea, in latitude 50°, and longitude 13°. It lies in the narrow valley of the Tepel, near its junction with the Eger. The population is 12,000, and the number of visitors about 40,000. The baths are open all the year, but are mostly resorted to in summer, from May to November. The climate is changeable, like that of all mountainous regions, and in spite of some smells in the lower part of the town, is claimed to be very healthy. No epidemics nor contagious diseases visit the place. The site is picturesque and the vicinity has good pine and spruce forest scenery. The mean summer temperature is 66° F., in the spring and autumn it is 47°. It is hot in summer like most mountain valleys. There are covered walks for the rainy days. The upper part, or Schlossburg, is the best location. The place is rather dear for Germany or even Austria, but the accommodations are good. People mostly take rooms and eat at the restaurants. The cure at Carlsbad is a serious one, and it is no place for those who wish to have a good time; yet there is good music and a theatre, with excellent performances. It is one of the most important springs in Europe as regards the gravity of the diseases sent to it, and while some of the French spas, as Vichy, have more visitors, Carlsbad waters are more active, and we must insist on great care being given to the diagnosis and to the patient's strength, and considerable caution being taken in their recommendation, as they are not to be played with.* A carefully directed course under the care of a local physician is essential, and we give a list of the competent physicians at the station, who all speak English.

Physicians. — Drs. London, Neubaur, Kraus, Hoffmeister, Grünberger, Rosenzweig, Ables, Gans, Strunz, Freund and Mayer.

After-cure.—This depends much on the patient; but mental and physical rest is usually insisted upon, and mountain air in Switzerland or Tyrol.

Hotels.— National, Victoria, Russie, Goldener Schild, Pupp's, König von England, Hannover. In June and July rooms should be engaged beforehand.

Local English Guides.—Carlsbad and its environs (Scribner's Sons.)

Bookseller.—Hans Feller.

English Church service at the new St. Luke's.

---

* Practitioners on the spot discriminate between the effects of the several springs, and this may be done at many other mineral water stations.

GIESSHÜBLER-PUCHSTEIN.

Our account of Carlsbad would not be complete if we failed to mention the Giesshübler Sauerbrunn. We have said elsewhere that Germany and Austria are lucky in having good spring water for table use, as the common rivers and streams are not wholesome. Giesshübler contains a good deal of iron, and therefore may not be suitable for every one ; but this acidulous, pleasant water is excellent for drinking purposes. The place itself is worth a visit, only nine miles from Carlsbad ; it is a capital drive along the banks of the Eger. The road passes through pine woods that are intersected with footpaths for the benefit of patients from Carlsbad.

FRANZENSBAD.

Route.—765 miles from Paris, E. of F. R.R., viâ Strasburg and Eger, thirty hours ; 110 francs. From London, £5 16s.

Waters.—There are nine cold springs of alkaline chloro-sulphated and iron waters,

but the great speciality here is the famous
Moorbäder or mud baths. The peaty ma-
terial used for these consists of sulphate of
potash and soda, with a little lime and phos-
phates of iron, and some organic matters.
A double bath is used, so that when the mud
one is over the patient steps into clean water.
The waters themselves of Franzensbad are
pleasant and agreeable, having a good deal
of carbonic acid gas in them. Baths of this
gas are also given. The treatment is laxative, diuretic, and of slightly exciting nature.

Therapeutics. — Anæmia and chlorosis,
chronic uterine complaints, sterility, neuralgia,
paralysis, hysteria ; skin diseases, such as
lichen, prurigo, urticaria, scrofula, rickets,
and hæmorrhoids in weak people.

Franzensbad, sometimes called Franzens-
brunnen, has an altitude of 1,560 feet, and a
population of but 1,200 ; with some 14,000
visitors, mostly of the female sex, during the
season. Chlorotic girls and pale women are
in the great majority here. The springs are
on an elevated plateau, but the country
around is not attractive, and has but little

of the beauty of Marienbad for instance. Living is very quiet, not to say dull, and is not cheap. The climate is cool, and owing to the elevation, is variable ; but it is healthy and airy. The park is a very fine one, and covered ways are provided for the rainy days, and for exercise. Some interesting promenades are those to Ludwigshöhe, Stodrerhöhe, and the ruins of Castle Eger.

English Church.—Service at the Hotel Königs-Villa.

Physicians.—Drs. Klein, Steinschneider, Egger, Loimann and Sommer.

Hotels.—Grand Hotel, Post, Hölzer, Hubner, Königs-Villa, and British Hotel.

MARIENBAD.

Route.—905 miles from Paris, E. of F.R.R., viâ Strasburg and Eger, thirty hours ; 115 francs. From London, £5 9s.

Waters.—There are eight cold alkaline-sulphated springs with iron, fifty-two degrees F. natural temp., heated for baths. The water is limpid, and without smell, giving a sharp salt taste, but is not very disagreeable.

It is called the cold Carlsbad, and it is much stronger in Glauber's salts than the last wells, but contains more iron, so that while it is more purgative than Carlsbad, it is tonic. It acts also as a diuretic, sudorific, aperitive, and it is considered sedative to the nervous system.

Therapeutics.—Obesity is the great speciality here, and all venous congestions : congestive headache, hæmorrhoids in strong subjects, catarrhal dyspepsia, syphilis, gout, gravel, biliary calculi, and intestinal obstruction ; female diseases.

After cure.—Great attention must be paid to diet after the cure for obesity, as the fat will return very rapidly.

Marienbad is in a beautiful broad valley, enclosed by pine clad hills, at altitude 1,912. The population is 2,000 ; number of visitors, 20,000.   It is only a short distance from Carlsbad.   The climate is that of central Germany, the barometer averaging 702.95 mm.   The air is fresh and bracing, but mild and constant in summer, during the season. The health of the place is excellent, and it seems protected from epidemics. It is a great station for corpulent men and women, but they give milk, whey, pine-cone, and carbonic gas baths, as well as the purgative water treatment. A new colonnade allows of exercise during wet days, and the electric light is now used in the town. There are many English and American visitors. There is a theatre and a fine concert hall, with good reading-rooms.

English and Scotch Church service.

The surrounding country is decidedly interesting. The top of the Podhorn, 2,750 feet, affords extensive views of the Bohemian forests, in which there are miles of delightful walks. Mecséry Temple and the Abbey of Tepl, nine miles out, must be seen as well as the Belvidere.

Physicians.—Drs. Lucca, David, Schindler-Barnay, Lucker.

Hotels. — Imperial, Weimar, Englischer Hof, Klinger and Casino.

(For fuller local information write to the *Bürgermeisteramt*.)

INDIFFERENT WATERS

Gastein.

Route.—748 miles from Paris, E. of F.R.R., viâ Munich to Lend; then drive through the Klamm-Pass for four hours, thirty-seven hours; 130 francs. From London, £6.

Waters.—They are simple thermal, or indifferent hot springs, and have no taste or smell. They are said, incorrectly, to contain electricity. They have but a minimum of mineral constituents; nevertheless they are a curious example of feebly mineralized water, having a real physiological action, producing strong sedation of the nervous system.

Therapeutics.—These waters are called the old folks' baths, as they seem to be the natural remedy for the decay of old age, and general debility. Nervous diseases, locomotor ataxy, impotence, spermatorrhœa, neuralgia, hysteria, hypochondria, and all forms of weakness.   Gout.

Contra-indications.—Fever and acute affections in general.

Bad Gastein.—This is a village of only forty-six houses, in the high Austrian Alps, Duchy of Salzburg ; at an altitude of 3,135 feet, between two mountains, the Graukogel, 7,800 feet, and the Stubnerkogel, 6,000 feet. There is a magnificent waterfall, height 270 feet, and very grand mountain scenery.   The climate is the result of the geographical situation.   For the last forty years Dr. Proell has taken meteorological observations, and his experience is that " Gastein has one of the coolest and most salubrious of climates." The showers are frequent, as is natural in the mountains, but they do not last long, and for use in this weather there are fine and large glass covered galleries.   The season is from May to September.   The walks are hilly, but care has been taken to put plenty of benches to rest upon.   Life is quiet here, as the frequenters are nervous and elderly people, and the object is soothing and seda-tive. There is good music.

Physicians.—Drs. Proëll (speaks English), Bunzel, Schneider.

Hotels. — Schloss, Strauberger, Hirsch, Grabenwirth.

N.B.—It is necessary to write some time ahead for rooms during the summer season.

Local Guides in English.—Consult Dr. Proëll's " Gastein, its Springs and Climate," C. Gerold's Son, Vienna, 1891.

TEPLITZ-SCHONAU.

Route.—820 miles from Paris, N. F.R.R., viâ Cologne and Dresden (five hours from Dresden), thirty-two hours; 124 francs. From London, £6.

Waters. — These thirteen hot alkaline springs (75° to 120° Fah.) contain some car-bonate of soda, and form another of the very remarkable group of indifferent waters, which, notwithstanding their feeble mineral-ization, give most excellent results in the treatment of disease. They are mostly used as baths, and every advantage is taken of the heat of the waters to act by stimulating the circulation, even causing revulsion. The mud or peat baths given help this action. Dax and Plombières in France resemble Teplitz.

Therapeutics.—From the above it will be seen that rheumatism, gout, stiffened joints, sciatica, anchylosis, &c., would be the diseases treated. They have also a reputation for gun-shot wounds and scrofulous gland swellings.

Teplitz or Töplitz.—This is a most popular Bohemian bath, and has been used for centuries. There are no less than nine large bath establishments. The word Teplitz is old Slavonic, meaning warm baths. It is in the valley of the Bela ; altitude, 700 feet ; population, 14,000. The visitors number some 30,000. of whom a large number are Russians. The village of Schönau is now one with Teplitz, and it is becoming popular, but it is rather a smoky place, by reason of the peat burnt in the factories. The town is not so dear as Carlsbad, and if it is small, it is lively, having a fine *Kurgarten*, a *Schloss-Gar-ten*, and concerts. The climate is pleasant in summer, although variable, but late and early in the season it is very cold. The table-waters used here are the famous Austrian Vichy waters, called Bilin and Krondorfer. The parks and gardens are fine, and the excursions into the Erz and Mittel mountains are interesting. Here we are near the curious and beautiful region called "Saxon Switzerland." *Eichwald* is near by also, where so many pulmonary invalids go for the air and milk cures. The Schlossberg, 1,280 feet in elevation, gives a fine view.

Physicians.—Drs. Kraus, Hirsch, Baumeister, Langstein, Lieblein, Mandel, and Stein.

Hotels.—Post, Roi de Prusse, London, Bahnhof, Kronprinz, and Schwarzes Ross. Prices vary with the season, and the custom is to charge by the week.

After-cure. — It is customary to advise going to the seaside after these baths, in order by using salt water bathing to harden the skin after the debility produced by the heat.

5

IRON-ARSENICAL WATERS.

LEVICO.

Route.—This place is reached by driving fifteen miles in three and a-half hours from *Trient*, a station on the Great Brenner Pass, R. R. between Verona and Innsbruck. £6 14s. from London.

Waters.—These extraordinary springs rise at Vetriolo, and similar waters are found at Roncegno, five miles from Levico. They contain arsenic, iron, and even copper, in large quantities, and are really strong mineral solutions, rather than waters as we usually understand them. They are dark in colour, and are given in tea and tablespoonful doses diluted in milk or plain water. They are even used for hypodermic injection, and are recognized in English therapeutical works.

Therapeutics. — Surprising results are claimed in anæmia, women's diseases, skin complaints, eczema, lichen, psoriasis, &c., as well as in malaria and rheumatism.

Levico is called the town of Trentin, and is about fifteen miles from Trent on the Brenta. Altitude 1,500 feet, population 7,000. It now has a new bath establishment, with eighty rooms and 120 marble baths. The baths are diluted, and vaseline is used afterwards to rub on the skin, such is the strength of the waters. The mud and grape cures are used here also. The season is June to September, and so far the place is cheap. It has been frequented by Italians, but from its importance is now visited by people of all nations. The excursions into Tyrol are very interesting. The cavern of St. Dominico at Vetriolo is 220 yards long, and the place is nearly 5,000 feet above sea-level.

Physicians. — Drs. Pacher and Arenini. Medical Director, Dr. Sartori.

Hotels.—Grand H. Cagliari, Bath's.

CLIMATIC HEALTH RESORTS.

Arco.

This pretty place is in Southern Tyrol, four miles from Riva, and is reached by the Brenner line from Innsbruck. £6 14s. from London. It is at the head of Lake Garda, and is sheltered by the mountains around it more than any place in Northern Austria. It claims to be a winter resort, and it certainly has a dry atmosphere, with a very small rainfall and absence of dust-storms, so that those who are in this part of Europe would be sure to find a better climate at Arco than in the rest of the Empire. It is indeed a bracing place, with a good amount of fair weather, but it must not be supposed to be warm. Compressed air treatment is used, as well as massage and electricity. Dr. Œrtel's exercise cure is well given here. The season is September to May.

Physicians.—Drs. Althammer, Schreiber, and Schilder.

Hotel.—Kurhaus-Arco.

ABBAZIA.

This station is on the Adriatic Sea, one hour by steam from *Fiume* in Dalmatia, and should be mentioned among the Austrian winter places. It is in the midst of beautiful scenery, and is suitable for diseases of the organs of respiration, at least in the autumn and spring. Of course none of these places claim a warm climate such as the Riviera in winter. It has only relative warmth and finer weather than the very cold Austrian cities.

Physicians.—Dr. von Hausen.

Hotel.—Grand Hotel Abbazia.

INNSBRUCK.

This station, on the Brenner line, is reached from Munich; population 24,000; the capital of Tyrol, 109 miles from Munich; altitude 2,000 feet. Fare £6 14s. from London. Its invigorating air is useful for invalids who

suffer from nervous debility, loss of sleep
and appetite. It claims to be a summer
and winter resort. Like other mountain
places it is crowded in July and August, but
a number of people remain all winter from
September to June. Swimming, salt baths,
and every comfort are to be had in the
Hotels Du Tirol, De l'Europe, and Goldene
Sonne; while theatres, balls, &c., give fair
amusement. We consider its best claim to
be a climatic station in summer for mountain
air, and it is useful before and after the season in the south.

Physicians.—Drs. Erendorfer, Glatz, Rokitansky, and Winkler.

MERAN.

The town of Meran is charmingly situated
in the valley of the Adige, and forms, with
the adjoining villages of Obermais and Un-
termais, a celebrated winter and spring health
resort. £7 11s. 6d. from London. It is
seventeen miles from Botzen, about twenty-
nine hours from Paris, 125 francs, twenty-

five from Berlin, and twenty from Vienna. The best approach is by Munich, thence to Innsbruck and Botzen. The altitude of Meran is 1,050 feet, that of Obermais is 1,200 feet. The place is protected by mountains that rise 10,000 feet above, and it is surrounded by grand old walnut and chestnut trees. Its climatic advantages are considerable. It may be said to be a cold, dry, well-sheltered tonic and sunny winter climate. It must not be supposed to be a warm place, as it has a pretty severe winter, but it is dry, having only fifty-five rainy days in the year, and only eleven in the winter. On a bright day, when the sun is shining, the temperature will mount to 60° Fahr., and one can go skating in a light coat. The mean temperature is 41°, 67° in winter. It has seven or eight days of snow, and is quite free from dust, while the winds are not strong. The population is 3,000, and number of visitors, 10,000. The sanitation is good, the death-rate only six per 1,000. It is the great place for the grape cure in September, and has a milk and whey cure in April, as well as an herb cure. Then a speciality is made of treatment by variations of air pressure in pneumatic air-chambers, in the Kurhaus, which is well-fitted with steam, electric and other baths. Massage is much used, and under Professor Oertel's direction, the gradual ascents, and the steep roads about the town have been marked off, numbered, and maps made of them to serve for his exercise cure.

Therapeutics.—Asthma, emphysema, phthisis (when the patient likes cold air, and is not subject to hæmoptysis), scrofula, gout, obesity, nervous diseases and convalescence.

Contra-indications.—Very old, weak and delicate people would certainly feel the cold here too much, and persons with weak circulation could not stand it.

Grape Cure.—Some two pounds of grapes daily are the usual treatment, but this is not so agreeable as it might seem. The fruit irritates the gums and mouth so that a weak solution of soda has to be used after eating them.

Physicians.—Drs. Braitenburg, Fischer,

Hirschfeld, Huber, Kittel, Kuhn, Ladurner, Proëll (of Gastein), Messing, Schreiber, and Veninger.

Hotels.—Habsburger Hof, Tyroler Hof, Erzherzog, Johann.

English Guide-Books.—Dr. Schreiber's " Meran, a Health Resort," and " Meran, Health Resort for Invalids " (Pötzelberger, printer, Meran).

VIENNA.

The capital city of Austria is 840 miles from Paris, 185 francs; forty-eight hours, 190 francs by R.R. From London, £8 4s. Its population is 1,250,000. It is in lat. 48° 13° N. Long. 16° 22° E. Its climate is cold in winter and hot in summer. Snow falls abundantly, and rain and frost are frequent, so that it cannot be recommended as a health resort. But the city has been greatly improved in late years by the erection of new hotels, gardens and squares, with wide streets that are well-lighted, cheerful and healthy. From a medical point of view Vienna is very important, owing to its splendid General Hospital in the Alserstrasse, with 2,500 beds, and many distinguished physicians. We give a list of Vienna's celebrated specialists whom patients may need to consult. Fees vary.

Surgeons.—Professor Billroth, Kolingasse, 6. Professor Albert, Maximilian-Platz, 7. Professor von Mosetig, Fleischmarkt, 1. Professor von Dittel, Alserstrasse, 4.

Physicians.—Professor Nothnagel, Rathausgasse, 13. Professor Oser. Dr. Drasche. Dr. Augustus Kosak, Nibelungen Gasse, 7.

Skin Diseases.—Professors Neumann and Kaposi. Dr. Hebra.

Eye Diseases.—Professor Fuchs. Professor Stellwag. Dr. Keuss.

Ear Diseases.—Professors Politzer and Grube. Dr. Bing.

Women's complaints. — Professors Chroback, Braun, Rokitansky.

Nervous Diseases.—Professor Benedict.

Children's Diseases.—Professors Widerhofer, Baron, Monti.

Throat Diseases.—Professors Schrotter and Chiari.

Baths and Hydrotheraphy.—Prof. Winternitz.

Hotels.—Imperial, Golden Lamb, Grand, Metropole, National, Continental, Archduke Charles.

Local Guides in English.—See Guides to Europe.

N.B.—See Physician's Directory for full list and addresses.

BELGIUM AND HOLLAND.

Belgium is between 40° 27′ and 51° 31′ N. lat., and 2° 37′ and 6° long.   It has a climate somewhat like England, but colder in winter, and with more frost and snow from November to April, while it is not so damp and foggy.   The mean temperature is 51°, with 197 wet days and sixty foggy ones.   The rainfall is about twenty-six inches.

Holland is lower than Belgium, and with its canals is marshy.   It is moist and foggy, while in winter the cold is considerable, the Zuider Zee being often frozen over.   158 wet days ; twenty-seven inches annual rainfall.

In these countries there are few watering-places that are frequented by English-speaking people.

IRON WATERS.

SPA.

Route.—248 miles from Paris, N. of F.R.R. ; eight hours ; forty-five francs ; three hours from Brussels. From London, viâ Dover, Lille, £3 2s. 6d.

The Waters.—These are cold, ferruginous, bi-carbonated, gaseous springs that have been known for ages. There are eight wells of clear, sparkling water, without special taste, which contain important ferruginous principles, making these springs one of the best iron waters in Europe. They are diuretic and chalybeate, and cause constipation. Peat and other baths are used.

Therapeutics.—Anæmia and chlorosis, leucorrhœa and functional utererine troubles, dyspepsia, hysteria, heart diseases.

Contra-indications.—Constipation, congestion and hæmorrhages.

Spa is in a deep valley on the Wayay, seventeen miles from Aix-la-Chapelle in Germany. It has fine walks on the pine-clad hills around it. The population is 25,000; there are 8,000 visitors; the altitude is 1,000 feet. The climate is good in fine weather, but the valley being low, whenever there is a storm around it is sure to settle over Spa. The season is May to October. The sanitation is excellent. The manufactories, which are so common in Belgium, are not found here. Notice the bread, which is even superior to that of Vienna. The baths are in a fine building, and they are among the most delightful in Europe. The clear sparkling water forms bubbles on the skin, and it seems like bathing in champagne. The walks are very good—long lanes that lead to the pine forests; the Promenade de Sept Heures, Allée le Marteau, Annette and Lubin mountains, Franchmont ruins, &c. Excellent horse-back riding can be done here on good ponies. Many English frequent the place.

English Church.—Rev. J. Harrison.

Scotch Church.—The Rev. — Affleck.

Physicians.—A. M. Cafferata* (English),
and Dr. de Damseau.

Hotels.—Bellevue, Flandre, York, Pays-
Bas, Des Bains, Brighton Hotel.

Bookseller.—J. Engel, opposite Pouhon
Spring.

English Book.—Dr. Cutler's Notes on
Spa.

---

* Dr. Cafferata is in Brussels in winter: 56, Rue
Crespel.

SEASIDE RESORTS.

OSTEND.

Fare from London, £1 11s. 3d. ; viâ Dover, direct steamer, 12s. 6d.

This sea bathing place is in West Flanders, on the North Sea, sixty miles east of Dover, and seventy-five miles from Brussels. The air is fine and bracing, while the sands are extensive, and every facility is afforded for good sea bathing in summer. The town is expensive, popular and fashionable. The King resides here in summer, and it is quite a resort for pleasure and amusement. There is an immense sea-wall or *digue* that forms a capital promenade. The population is 25,000, and there are as many as 60,000 visitors from June to the end of September.

English Church.—Rue Longue.

Physicians.—Drs. Gerard, Janssen and Van Dyl.

Hotels. — Continental, Fontaine, Great Ocean, Kursaal, Marion and Plage.

HOLLAND.

Seaside.—Scheveningen.

These sea baths are the only ones that are much known to our people, and indeed the only resort that we feel called upon to mention in the country. They have a fine sandy beach, and the place is three miles from the Hague. There is a magnificent *Kursaal*, and Grand Hotel, *Kurhaus*. The fine orchestra of eighty musicians is from Berlin. It shares with Ostend in being aristocratic and dear. It must not be forgotten that the country is a rainy one, so bring plenty of waterproofs along.

Physicians.—Drs. Fracken, Mess.

FRANCE.

The climate of France is temperate. In the north it resembles that of Great Britain, but it is not quite so rainy. The centre has a model temperate climate, while the south has a mild atmosphere similar to that of Florida.

The lat. is between 42° 32′ and 51° 5′ north. Rain falls on about 140 days; the mean annual temperature is 51° in the north. The south has 110 rainy days, and a mean annual temperature of 58°. Paris has a variable climate with a mean annual temperature of 51°; 147 rainy days, and seventeen days with snow or hail. The snow never lies long, certainly not over one day in the city parts. There is but little fog. In this respect, and as to its climate in general, Paris is much superior to London.

France is the most highly endowed country in Europe in the matter of health resorts, containing as it does over 1,000 mineral spring stations, many of them with very complete arrangements and great reputation, as well as many celebrated winter and seaside resorts. Many of the mineral water places add " Les Bains " to the name to distinguish it from the town, or from other places in the country having a similar name. Very often the village called by the name is a few miles

6

from *Les Bains* or the Baths. Or again, "Les Eaux," "the waters," after a name is used for the same purpose, and also refers to places where the waters are mostly employed as a drink, and not so much for bathing purposes.

SULPHURETTED SPRINGS.

AIX-LES-BAINS. (SAVOY, FRANCE.)

Routes and Fares. — From Paris by P. L. M. R. R., viâ Macon, 361 miles. The 9 p.m. express takes nine hours, arriving at 6.30 a.m. The 8.55 a.m. day express arrives at 7.14 p.m., both without change of cars.

First class fares are 65 francs (13 dollars, £2 12s.). Second-class is 44 francs (8 dollars, £1 15s. 6d.). The trains have second-class carriages.

Geneva.—Viâ Culoz, is three hours train. Ten francs (8s., 2 dollars), first-class.

Turin.—Direct by train, is six hours, 25 francs (5 dollars, £1), first-class.

London is eighteen hours in all, sixteen-and-half train and one hour and a-half stop in Paris. Fare, first-class, 137 francs (27 dollars, £5 10s.).

The fashionable and popular watering

place called Aix-les-Bains (pronounced "Ex-lay-Ban") is on the great railway line Paris to Italy and Switzerland.

It is situated in the middle of a large and picturesque valley in the Alpine Savoy district of France. Its altitude is 823 feet above sea level, and 90 feet above Lake Bourget.

The town is surrounded by hills and mountains of easy ascent. On the south is Mont Grenier with the Chartreuse Monastery. On the west is the Dent du Chat (Cat's Tooth Mountain) while to the east is the Grand Revard and Nivolet Mountains.

Aix is a pleasant and healthy place of residence, large sums having been spent in drainage works, and in supplying the town with pure water. The sanitation is excellent, owing to the great quantity of water coming from the overflow of the baths which is used for flushing the sewers. It is also on this account that there are no disagreeable exhalations remarked like those in many of the sulphur spring stations. The climate is soft and mild. The average temperature being 55° F. during the year. The mean summer temperature is 70° F., but occasionally it rises as high as 78° to 80° F., in July and August. This heat is felt very much by the English, who come from a damp cold climate, but most Americans would think very little of such a temperature, as they have it much hotter in summer at home. June and September are delightful months at Aix-les-Bains. The thermometer then ranges from 65° to 70° F., and the air is bright, pleasant and sunny. The vegetation of this part of Savoy is nearly the same as the south of France, but the air is not so dry. The near-by mountains cause a certain number of showers in summer, just as in all high regions. There is a marked difference between Aix and the Riviera as regards sleeping. Owing to the excellent atmospheric conditions people rest well here, while in the south the exciting air tends to produce insomnia in nervous patients. There is no cretinism or gôitre seen in Aix, like that of the Swiss Mountains. The population is about 6,000, but nearly 35,000 visitors come here during the year besides the regular residents.

With these healthy conditions, and its valuable mineral waters, whose curative properties are now so well-known, we must add the beauty of its scenery, mountain and lake climate, with the change to pure air and rest from work, as valuable adjuncts to the treatment at Aix.

The Waters of Aix-les-Bains.

Like many other mineral spring stations in Europe, this one was known and used by the Romans in ancient times, many relics are found of their occupation of the place.

The springs are *Sodio-Calcareo-Sulphuretted hot ones* two in number, having a temperature of 114° to 117° F. One of the springs was called "*The Alum,*" but they differ very little in quality, and may be considered and used as one. They yield over one million gallons of water daily, and its most important chemical elements are: Sulphuretted Hydrogen; Carbonic acid and free Nitrogen gas; Hyposulphites and Carbonates of Calcium, with some Chlorides. Finally, we must mention the existence, or possibly the production of electricity during the use of the baths. There are traces also of Iodides and Bromides in the waters of these springs, as well as other substance, such as the curious organic matter called "*Barégine.*" The water is easy of digestion, but Aix is not the usual water drinking station seen in many places, where boys and maidens dressed in fancy costumes, hand up glasses of mineral water to eager patients. The water here is so plentiful that it is allowed to flow freely from public fountains, where it can be drunk gratis. There is also a special Spigot in the bath establishment where the water comes direct from the springs. It must not be supposed that this free drinking precludes the use of the water internally. It is considered highly beneficial to drink the hot sulphur waters of Aix. English medical writers speaking of the use of mineral waters say that springs of the class of Aix have the advantage of being thermal, or hot, and act on the system by diluting the blood temporarily, and lowering the percentage of urates, and sodium salts. This tends to retard uratic precipitation and gives the kidneys time to overtake their arrears in the task of eliminating uric acid. We shall not dwell here on the therapeutic action produced by drinking the Aix waters, except to say that it is certainly powerful in its good influence over disease.

LOCAL VAPOUR BATHS.

The Thermal Establishment.—This handsome massive stone bath house is one of the finest in Europe. It belongs to the French Government, and is under the Ministry of the Interior, who also direct the Hygiene, and Public Assistance departments in France. The building contains two immense swimming baths called "*Piscines;*" four smaller swimming baths, about fifty single baths, fifty douche rooms with massage, six "*Bouillons,*" or vapour rooms, five "*Etuves,*" or hot dry air rooms, two "*Caisses,*" or general vapour baths, and four local vapour applications called "*Berthollet's.*"

Some 2,000 douches and 1,000 baths can be, and often are, given daily during the season. The pressure of the water varies according to the height of the bath in the building. The ground floor ones having fourteen metres; first floor, nine, and the second floor, six metres ; so that the doctors have at their command pressure, temperature (hot and cold to a degree), with a complete set of hydrotherapeutic apparatus.

The Douche Massage.—One of the most important applications of the Aix waters is the massage or shampooing of the patient while under the hot sulphur water. This is done here with a perfection that does not exist elsewhere in the world. The men and women who perform it have had their art handed down to them for many years, as their fathers and mothers have been "*mas-seurs*" or "*masseuses*" before them. The Aix waters have an unctuous quality which makes them particularly adapted to rubbing and kneading the muscular structures that is not found in other waters.

THE DOUCHE MASSAGE.

The *Douche-Massage* is given as follows :—
The patient is placed on a wooden stool, and the attendants pour the water over the body from a hose while, at the same time, they shampoo, knead and rub according to

the directions given by the physician who accompanies the patient to the douche the first time to give instructions as to temperature, force, duration and pressure on particular parts. This speciality of massage under water has nothing in common with the dry massage or that practised with ointments elsewhere.

Whey and milk cures, and electricity by the use of the continuous current, is often combined with the Aix and Marlioz mineral water treatment. The indications as to diet vary so much during the course and with each patient, that only a physician, after a thorough examination of every case, can properly give correct diet tables.

The Bath Chairs.—Another speciality of this station is the carrying home of the patient after the douche. The custom is to walk to the bath house (although the patient may be carried to it if desired); the hotel servant carries a blanket and linen to the establishment, which is furnished without extra charge by the hotels. The bather having disrobed in the dressing room attached to the douche, enters the bath, and the usual clothing is returned to the hotel by the servant. After the douche and rubbing down, the patient is carefully wrapped in the blanket, which has been warmed in a gas oven in the meantime, and the bath chair having been brought into the dressing room, the patient is put into it, and carried to the hotel, up to his room,

THE BATH CHAIRS.

where he is deposited in bed and left to perspire a certain time, when he is again rubbed down by the attendant, or by himself, and resumes his usual attire in time for breakfast.

This we consider an important part of the Aix treatment. How much harm is done and how many colds are caught elsewhere by the usual method of taking baths and then dressing quickly in hot dressing rooms, and walking home with the pores of the skin open, while the weather may be cold or wet.

Marlioz.

These important sulpho-sodic and bromo-iodurated mineral water springs, are really within Aix-les-Bains itself, as Marlioz is only fifteen minutes' walk by a fine shaded avenue, while tramways run to it constantly. It is situated within a pretty park in the suburbs of Aix. The springs are three in number, and they are compared to the sulphur waters of the Pyrenees, like *Eaux Bonnes*, but they are stronger in mineral elements than this spring. The temperature is 57° F., and they yield 50,000 quarts daily. The establishment contains two inhalation rooms, ten fine spray apparatus, nasal and pharangeal douches, and a good bathing department.

It is here that the throat and nose troubles are treated with those of the respiratory organs mentioned under " Diseases Successfully Treated."

These waters form a most valuable adjunct

to the other courses of treatment given in
Aix. Owing to the alkalinity of the Marlioz
waters, drinking them has an important influence upon the treatment of gout and rheumatism, because of their alkaline action on
the bladder, perspiration and the other secretions. Chlorosis and anæmia often derive
more benefit from this class of sulphur waters
than they do from the pure iron springs.

CHALLES AND ST. SIMON.

Challes is reached from Chambéry which
is twenty minutes by rail from Aix. A tramway runs out to the station from the last-
named town in half-an-hour. The cold
sulphur waters of Challes are among the
strongest known. They are supplied at Aix
at the chemists, or drug stores from fountains, and this water is used by Aix phy
sicians in conjunction with the Aix treatment
in certain diseases, especially skin and scrofulous affections. They should be taken in
very small quantities at a time, owing to their
strong mineral properties.

St. Simon is a mineral spring in the

environs of Aix, about a mile out on the other side, on what is called the Geneva Road. It contains a small quantity of lime and magnesia and is used for drinking only, in certain bladder troubles.

Diseases successfully treated at Aix-les-Bains and Marlioz.—We give here a simple enumeration only, while stating that it is the *chronic* forms of maladies that should be sent here, we leave to the home physician the task of judging each special case.

First, all the chronic articular and muscular forms of rheumatism. All torpid and lymphatic diseases. Neuralgia, sciatica, lumbago, pleurodynia, nodosity of joints, rheumatic gout, and gout of a chronic articular nature. Gonorrhœal rheumatism, skin diseases, such as eczema, acne, lichen, psoriasis, prurigo, syphilis. Surgical troubles, such as old sprains, fractures, firearm wounds, atrophy and retraction of muscles. Paralysis, both local, hysterical and lead forms. Hemiplegia and paraplegia. Chronic catarrhal affections, laryngitis, pharyngitis, rhinitis, ozæna, herpes of pharynx, bronchitis, asthma, as well as the catarrhs of the digestive, uterine and urinary passages, women's diseases, amenorrhœa, dysmenorrhœa, vaginitis, hæmatocele, metritis, leucorrhœa, and change of life, diabetes, obesity, myxœdema, anæmia, and chlorosis, neurasthenia, ataxia, hysteria and certain forms of other nervous troubles.

The Therapeutical Action of the Waters of Aix-les-Bains.—The wonderful cures obtained here are explained as follows :—

There is produced an energetic stimulation of the cutaneous surface which results as it were in a purgation of the skin, making it eliminate whatever excrementitious matters that have been retained in the organism. It also relieves at the same time, any congestion of the deeper parts or organs, while giving a stimulus to the circulation in general. To this must be added the effects of the mineral elements in the waters taken into the system and blood, both by drinking and inhaling them during the bath or douches.

We must add a word of warning to

patients who are disposed to take these powerful massage douches without advice, as harm can result from an injudicious use of them. Some people insist on the Masseurs giving them a vigorous treatment when they have no proper power of reaction, so that they simply exhaust themselves and produce a state of feverish debility and weakness, whilst under proper medical direction the same persons could derive great benefit from the Aix waters scientifically used.

Best Season for the Course, and its Duration.—The bathing establishment is open all the year round, but the Aix doctors do not advise patients to come here before May nor to remain after October. English visitors rather prefer cold weather, and they often arrive for the baths in May, and return again in September. Americans come during the whole season, but prefer the summer. The most fashionable and crowded time is during July and August. This is true of all the mineral springs of Europe, and the question may be asked if the world in general is right in flocking in thousands to the baths

7

during the hot months? Certainly severe rheumatic cases, old people, and those sensitive to cold, must find it best for them to come at this time, or they would not do so in such great numbers. We now have the fresh air and oxygen of the neighbouring heights within easy reach by the Revard R. R. so that it is possible to escape from the occasional hot days of the valley when not endurable, and the nights are always pleasant in Aix. The months of May, June and September, have certain advantages ; the baths are not so crowded, the air is more bracing, and reasonable rates prevail.

As to the duration of the treatment : it has been rather arbitrarily fixed by custom, at three weeks, or twenty-one days, and many take about sixteen douches in this time, with one or two days' rest between, but this should all depend upon the case. Almost every patient demands a careful study by a competent bath physician who alone can fix the proper duration and number of douches.

It may be said, though in a general way,

that many people get sufficient treatment in three weeks. Some cases require two seasons to cure a chronic malady, but all get improvement in a single one. It is important that the baths and douches be not taken continuously, brief intervals of rest are essential to success in the treatment. This is the experience of the best physicians who have practised for many years at this station. An " *after cure* " of some little time in a cool mountain resort, such as we now have on the Grand Revard Mountain, is always advisable.

The Mont Revard : its Double Cog-wheel Railway.—Notwithstanding the many attractions of Aix, it was still considered not quite perfect by some. The Massage treatment is of itself an energetic exercise, putting as it does into action many muscles that we do not use in ordinary walking. The result is that a certain amount of fatigue is felt after the douche-massage, and many patients are not disposed to walk or take other exercise. Besides this in midsummer from the topographical position of the town, which we have already spoken of, it occasionally has an elevated temperature which is trying to certain patients, while at the same time very favourable to their treatment as they are mostly sensitive rheumatic people.

It was felt that some change of air between the douches would be of advantage, at least for those who accompany the patients. And these combined causes made all to look with longing eyes to the tops of the high mountains around, where pure cool air was known to prevail. This led to the idea of a mountain railway like that of the Rhigi, and other places in Switzerland.

The Grand Revard Mountain towers over Aix some 4,400 feet, and its summit is 5,100 feet above the sea level. A continuous double cog-wheel railway was built to its summit and was opened in August, 1892. It carried over 1,200 visitors up to the top during the first two weeks it was running, and it is certainly destined to great success in the future. The total length of the line is 9,200 meters, or about six miles; the journey up takes about an hour, but there are stations every fifteen minutes at different heights.

The slope is a very gradual one, being 1 in 22 at the most, or about 16 per cent., while the Rhigi is 25, and the Pilatus is 48. The system is Abt's, that is, a double line of steel cogs between the rails that lock into the centre wheel of the inclined steam engine or locomotive, thus giving perfect safety. The line on the Rhigi, which, as we have said above, is much steeper than this one, has been in use for 22 years without a single accident. This new railway will not only be useful to those who wish to go up and pass a day at its summit, where there is an immense plateau from which they can enjoy a view of Mont Blanc, with a superb panorama of the other mountain ranges, but its several stations on the road will permit of using any desired altitude in the treatment of disease.

The idea of a railway up this mountain was advocated by some physicians at Aix who saw the advantage of having a climatic station as well as a thermal one here. Already ground has been taken up at Pugny Station on this line, at an elevation of 2,000 feet, at a spot where no fogs come, for the establishment of a *Hotel-Sanatorium*. Here the "*air cure*" can be given in all its perfection. In making use of this grand therapeutical measure it is considered that a gradual transition to high ground is necessary. Aix already is 823 feet above sea level, Pugny is 2,000 feet, and the summit of the Revard 5,000 feet. Careful studies have been made by physicians and other scientific men as to the meteorological conditions of the Revard for several years past, and this mountain has been found to possess superior advantages for the air cure to the well-known climatic stations in Germany, located in the damp hills of the Taunus, and in the Black Forest, where notwithstanding the bad climate, excellent results have been constantly obtained in the treatment of disease by air. It is therefore certain that under the good conditions found on the grand Revard, such as proper elevation, pure mountain air, protection from wind, splendid water supply, sunny exposition, and gravelly soil, that this Alpine region, situated as it is in the mild climate of central France, only nine hours from Paris, is destined to become a most important mountain health resort.

We do not at this time enter into its many medical indications, but we wish to add that Aix is no longer dependant on its neighbour Switzerland for a mountain "*after cure*," for not only is it now possible to combine the pure high mountain air cure with the hot sulphur treatment of Aix, but also a stay can be made in the tonic air on these piny heights which are free from microbes, in place of taking fatiguing journeys elsewhere. The railway company have bought some hundreds of acres of the pine forest on the summit, which is laid out in a park, and they have erected a grand hotel in the Swiss style, with spacious rooms. The views from the verandahs are of unsurpassed beauty. The walks and promenades on this great mountain plateau are numerous and beautiful. The villages of Bauges, St. François, Le Noyc, Tour de l'Anglais, and Mont Cluse must be seen to be appreciated properly.

THE CASINOS OF AIX-LES-BAINS.

Aix has still many more attractions. It is very different to the thousand and one little villages all over Europe, that have Mineral Springs but are *insufferably dull.* This bright little town has two splendid Casinos or Opera Houses combined with Clubs; Music and Ball Rooms as well as Reading Saloons where all the newspapers of the world are found on the tables. The most brilliant, fashionable and gay society throng these rooms, while the best music, operas and plays are performed in them daily. There are also the finest *Baccara* Saloons where ladies are admitted, as well as gentlemen.

The Cercle.—This Casino is the oldest, having been founded in 1824. It is a very fine building. The theatre having become too small for the large number of frequenters to it, a new one is now being built that will cost a million of francs. The concerts here are conducted by M. Colonne, with his celebrated Paris Orchestra. These are followed by grand operas or comedies on the off nights, with the best prima donnas and artists from the great theatres of Europe. There is also a capital Punch and Judy Show for the children, and frequent illuminations with fireworks of the large park attached to the Cercle.

The Villa Des Fleurs.—This club and theatre is situated in a pretty garden below the Cercle. Its baccara rooms are said to be the best decorated ones in Europe. Both of these casinos have free billiard rooms, fencing saloons, croquet, swings, and other games attached to them. They are open from May to October.

While the two theatres of the Casinos are large enough for the wants of a great city, it must not be supposed that Aix is a large place. It is still a country town, and a few minutes takes one out of the streets into pretty walks up the hills, or down to one of the ports of the beautiful Lake Bourget, where steamers provide pleasant excursions on the lake, and the boats good fishing. The mountain drives are varied and charming. Large brakes leave the Place Revard daily, and take one for a very reasonable sum to the *Dent du chat* mountain top ; to *Gorger de Fier, Hautecombe, Moulin de Prime, La Chambotte ;* while *Chambéry, Challes* and the famous *Chartreuse Convent* are only extensions of these beautiful drives.

An excellent race course open in July and August, and pigeon-shooting matches, with lawn tennis in the city park, provides the attractions dear to robust people.

The hotels of Aix are numerous and varied ; new ones are being constantly added, while furnished apartments can be had in private villas. Prices are much the same here as elsewhere in Europe ; good board being found from about 10 francs (dols. 2), 8s., per day, and less by taking rooms and private houses and providing oneself with food from the excellent daily market. As to the grand hotels, they are some of the finest in Europe, and their charges are like those of the rest of the continent, being in proportion to the ac-

commodation given.   Early in the season
and late, there is always a reduction of rates.
An English Church and Presbyterian Chapel
exist in Aix, with regular Sunday service
during the season.

French doctors do not as a rule speak
other languages, but Aix is an exception, as
almost all of its excellent practitioners speak
English.   We give a list of them—Drs.
Bertier, Blanc, Brachet, Cazalis, Coze, Fran-
con, Forestier, Guilland, Legrand, Mace,
M'Roe, Petit, and Vidal.   Stanley-Rendal
(E.).

American.—Thomas Linn, M.D., Place
Centrale 115.

Hotels. — De l'Europe, Grand, Nord,
Metropôle, Continental, Damesin, Louvre,
Beau-Site, Splendid, Venat Bristol, Chateau
Durieux, and many others.

Restaurants.—At the Cercle, and " London
House " at the Villa des Fleurs.

Booksellers.—Bolliet, Mermoz. Dr. Brachet
has a complete work in English on the waters,
and nearly all the other doctors have monographs on the subject.

BRIDES-LES-BAINS (SAVOY).

466 miles from Paris, P.L. M.R.R. to Albertville, changing at Chambéry, one and a half hours; 73 francs. From London, £6. From Albertsville station, twenty miles by bus, in three hours, to Brides (pronounce (*Breed*). The R. R. will be open to *Moutiers*, in July, 1893, half an hour by omnibus.

The Waters.—They are sulphato-chlorinated, and warm (95°F.) containing a good deal of carbonic acid gas. They are slightly styptic in taste, and somewhat acid. Their properties are tonic and restorative, and laxative when taken in a certain quantity. They are also diuretic, and stimulate the digestive functions.

Therapeutics.—Obstinate constipation, catarrh of urinary passages, diabetes, uterine diseases, congestion of liver, obesity; malaria of hot climates.

Brides claims to be a sort of French Carlsbad, but its waters are not so purgative. The town is situated on the Tarentaise or Upper Savoy mountains, close to Switzerland; and it is quite as good a mountain resort as many in this last country. The climate is fresh and bracing. The season is from May to October; the station is not now difficult of access, and the value of its waters warrants its being more used than it is. The altitude is 1,870 feet above sea. The place, on the banks of the River Doron, is very pretty. There is some good fishing. It has also a good casino with music, and a lawn tennis ground. Salins-Moutiers is only two miles off, with its saline springs, like those of Kreuznach and Nauheim, used for scrofulous children.

Physicians.—-Drs. Delastre, Desprez and Philibert.

Hotels.—Grand Hotel Des Thermes (has English Church service), Hotel de France, De Brides.

Books.—Drs. Delastre and Desprez have monographs on the Waters in English, and Dr. Philibert one on Obesity. The doctors speak English.

ALLEVARD (ISÈRE).

417 miles from Paris, P.B. M.R.R. to Gonçelin, fourteen hours; 75 francs. From

Gonçelin station to Allevard, by omnibus in one hour. Altitude, 1,550 feet. From London, £5 14s. 6d.

The Waters.—They are warm (73° Fah.), Calcaro-sulphuretted, giving 882,000 gallons per day from one well, in which all the waters centre. They have a stronger smell than the Aix waters, and the taste is bitter and astringent; but patients get accustomed to it very rapidly. Indeed, it is astonishing that people so soon get used to drinking all sorts of mineral water; it is rare that any one gives up the treatment at any spring, owing to the impossibility of taking the waters. This spring is compared by some writers to Eaux-Bonnes in the Pyrénées in regard to its action on the circulation and nutrition. It acts especially on the mucous membranes and the skin, and contains more carbonic acid gas than most of the sulphur springs. There is a milk and whey cure here also.

Therapeutics.—Chronic inflammations of the throat and larynx, with nasal catarrh, skin diseases, asthma, leucorrhœa, phthisis.

Contra-indications.—Like most high mountain places, this has a cold morning and evening temperature.

Allevard, on the River Breda, is in the midst of grand mountains, only twenty-three miles from Grenoble, with beautiful scenery and fine excursions to be made on every hand. Population 3,000. The climate is mild as compared to Paris, but not so damp. Excursions to Bout du Monde, Pont du Diable, 2,185 feet, Sept Lacs, Glacier du Glayzin, 9,200 feet.

Physicians.—Drs. Isoard and Niepce.

Hotels.—Du Louvre, de la Planta, des Alpes, des Bains.

URIAGE (ISÈRE).

403 miles. P.L.M. R.R. (Gare de Lyon) to Gières (near Grenoble), in thirteen and a half hours ; 74 francs. £5 16s. Then a half-hour's drive in omnibus to Uriage.

The Waters.—They are mixed sulphuro-chlorinated tepid springs (80° Fah.). There is also an iron water spring, but the saline sulphur one is the important spring of the station. It is a clear water ; it becomes turbid on standing, and gives a precipitate of a portion of the sulphur. The taste is like most sulphur waters, but is also salt. The waters resemble those of Aix-la-Chapelle. In doses of two glasses per day they are laxative, and four to six such doses act as a purgative. They are also tonic and strengthening, while they produce a marked sedative action on the nervous system. The spring is under a covered glass gallery, where the drinkers can take exercise in rainy weather.

Therapeutics.—Scrofula, ozona, otorrhœa, caries, necrosis, syphilis, rickets, certain nervous diseases, chronic catarrhs, rheumatism, eczema, acne, &c., and congestions of liver. Many children are treated here.

Uriage is really a suburb of Grenoble, being only eight miles from that city. It is one of the pretty valleys seen in the Dauphinese Alps ; altitude 1,350 feet. It is a very small place: Nearly all the buildings belong to the company, and they are divided off into hotels of various classes, prices varying from nine to fifteen francs and upwards per day. The climate is mild, and the place much crowded in the season—May to October. There is a handsome "Cercle" where balls and concerts go on all the season. The excursions are some of the finest in this splendid mountain region. See the Montagne des Quatre Seigneurs, 3,094 feet, in an hour and a-half; fine view; Château d'Uriage, Grenoble itself.

Physicians.—Drs. Doyon, Zenlow, Valio (French).

Hotels.—Write "Directeur de l'Etablissements," Uriage.

BAGNÈRES DE BIGORRE (HAUTE PYRÉNÉES).

523 miles from Paris, Orleans and S. of F.R.R., viâ Bordeaux, direct, all rail, twenty-two hours, ninety-six francs. From London, £7 1s.; altitude 1,860 feet.

Waters.—They are various; a number of them are iron and arsenical springs, with a faint quantity of sulphides. There are no less than fifty wells at Bagnères of different degrees of heat, 72° to 82° Fah., including the valuable rich sulphurous spring called *Labassère.* The other are saline, ferruginous and arsenical. The hotter ones are slightly stimulating and exciting, and the others are somewhat diuretic. The place is useful for hyper-sensitive people, and its therapeutic indications are very extensive.

Therapeutics.—Anæmia, chlorosis, uterine troubles, sterility, leucorrhœa, dyspepsia, chorea, nervous exhaustion, irritable heart, sleeplessness, gastralgia, paralysis, neuralgia, hysteria, and many cases of gout are also benefited.

Bagnères is a large place for a mineral spring station, so many of them being small country villages. Here we have a city of 12,000 inhabitants, with a permanent town, somewhat Spanish looking in appearance. Formerly many of the English who reside abroad made it a place where they stayed all the year round, and it has a pretty English church, built in 1859. This fell into decay, but during the last few seasons, since they have had an English doctor, many English families have returned to Bagnères. It does not, however, deserve the name of a winter resort so much as other places in this region; but it has a mild, bracing climate in a charming situation on the banks of the Adour, in the beautiful valley of Campan, overlooking the rich plain of Tarbes, free from cold winds. It is not in the high Pyrenean mountains, but just where they begin to rise from the plains, extending down to the Bay of Biscay. The residents of Pau come here a great deal in winter, and more in summer, with many French and Spanish people. The mean temperature is 46° 5′; the rainy days are 147. It is less humid than Pau and the rest of this country.

The winter months are clear, dry, bright, and slightly frosty.

It has a reputation for the cure of insomnia. A French savant who was cured here says its name should be changed from Bagnères de Bigorre to "*Ici on dort*"—here one sleeps.

It is a particularly clean town, and is a cheerful residence for a long or a short stay. There is a fine casino and plenty of music. The excursions are excellent ; most attractive walks abound. See Coustous, Allée Maintenon and Lourdes, with its curious statue of the Virgin ; and make the ascent to the

Pic du Midi, the highest meteorological station in Europe, 9,445 feet, going by Barèges. Although so high, the ascent can be made in about four hours on horseback.

English Church.—The Rev. T. Grundy.

Physician.—(E.) Dr. Middleton.

Bookseller.—L. Père, Place Strasbourg.

Hotels.— De Paris, Beau Séjour, France, Thermal.

BARÈGES.

This station must be mentioned as it gives the well-known name in France to all sulphur baths which are known as Bains de Barèges, no matter where taken. We refer now to the many sulphur baths given at home in the cities, and which are made by putting into any water a chemical sulphur compound, and thus creating an artificial bath of Barèges. The place itself, like many others that have given a name to something, is not at all frequented—like Castile soap that is made in Marseilles, and not at Castile. The truth is, that Barèges is a barren village about five hours' drive from Bagnères, over the Col de Tourmalet — the highest carriage drive in the Pyrénées, and one of the highest in Europe (7,000 feet above the sea). It can be more easily approached from Luz Station or Pierrefitte, by a four hours' drive.*   Its situation is dreary, presenting nothing interesting, but it is an ancient mineral spring that was well-known to Julius Cæsar. Louis XIV. established a military hospital here, and soldiers are still sent to Barèges to be treated. The speciality is old wounds and traumatic affections, with bone diseases and scrofula, as well as old sprains.

Physician.—Dr. Grimaud.

Hotels.—Des Princes, France, Richelieu.

CAUTERETS (HAUTES PYRÉNÉES).

540 miles from Paris.   Orléans R.R., viâ Bordeaux to Pierrefitte, on S. of F.R.R. Then, bus or carriage for seven miles drive up in two hours.   Eighteen and half hours, R.R., 98 francs.   From London, £7.

Waters.—They are sodio-sulphuretted hot and warm springs that are clear in colour but smell like all the sulphur waters. They are thought to be milder and more soothing in their action than Luchon, for instance.

---

* M. Taine said of Barèges " One must have plenty of good health to get cured here." The climate is very variable, great heat alternating with sharp, cold mists.

One spring, the Mahourat, is considered of great efficacy in dyspepsia.

Therapeutics. — Among its twenty-four wells, the great speciality of the place is La Raillière, which is considered a cure for all chronic inflammations of the throat and the air passages. It is used also for phthisis, catarrhs of the stomach, urethral discharges, spermatorrhœa, and many other diseases.

Cauterets (pronounced Cottray), population 2,000, is an ancient health resort that had almost been forgotten, but in late years has become very popular. The patients who are there are really ill, and lose no time in pleasure, but carry out the treatment with much care, and the doctors give the waters with the greatest precaution. The gay gambling set that we see at Luchon and Aix are not here. Many actors and actresses, though, like Sarah Bernhardt and others, have the greatest faith in the waters, and come here yearly for the treatment. There are over 25,000 visitors during the summer season, June to September. The village itself is small; altitude, 3,050 feet; it is in a narrow valley between high mountains.   The climate, as in all such places, is changeable, and rather damp from the constant storms.   It is well not to go up too early, as snow is often seen in early June.   In all cases take warm clothing, as the evenings and mornings are cold. There is the usual casino with large reading-rooms, &c.

Excursions.—To Lac de Gaube, 5,870 feet, in three hours ; Pont d'Espagne ; the Spanish border, &c.

Physicians.—Dr. Dehourcau (speaks English), Drs. Bordenave and Flurin.

Hotels. — Continental, France, d'Angleterre, Paris.

Bookseller.—A. Gazaux.

EAUX BONNES (BASSES PYRÉNÉES).

446 miles from Paris, Orléans R.R. Bordeaux and S. of F.R.R., to Laruns station, then carriage half-an-hour, sixteen hours ; 96 francs.   From London, £6 16s.

Waters.—Warm sulphur springs.   These " Good Waters " come from seven springs at a temperature of 90° Fah. They are clear, rather oily to the feel, and have the usual sulphur or bad-egg smell ; yet the flavour is sweetish, so that it is drunk without repugnance. The quantity is limited, and not many baths are taken. The waters are mostly used internally, and by spray or gargling. A speciality is made of hot foot-baths as a revulsion (Dr. Pidoux).

Therapeutics. — The principal maladies treated here are complaints of the chest, throat, larynx, and respiratory organs ; phthisis, torpid form ; chronic bronchitis.

After Cures.—It is quite common in France to recommend patients who are delicate in the throat or chest to pass the summer at these sulphur waters, and the winters at one of the resorts on the Riviera, while a short time may be passed in the interval at the seaside.

Les Eaux Bonnes (pronounced *O-Bun*) is at an elevation of 2,460 feet, surrounded by lofty mountains, in the valley of Ossau. It is a quiet, agreeable place, frequented by the seriously ill. It may be recommended as an air cure. There is the usual casino and band of music, reading-room, &c. The climate, while a mountain one, is considered soothing, as there is but little wind except during the thunderstorms, which are inevitable in high mountain places. .

The excursions are one to the Horizontal Promenade, a sort of balcony on the side of the hill, then to the Jardin Anglais, and many other points in the dark pine-woods around. The place is frequented by priests and clergymen for the cure of sore throat. Actors and singers also abound here, but not many English people, although it is only twenty-four miles from Pau.

Physicians.—Drs. Cazaux, Cazenave de la Roche.

Hotels.—Des Princes, France, Poste, Europe, Paix.*

LUCHON (HAUTE GARONNE).

737 miles from Paris, Orléans R.R. S. of F. direct; nineteen hours; ninety-three francs.

---

* *Eaux Chaudes* is only six miles by a good carriage road, but this "Hot Water" is not used, in fact, it is almost deserted. It is a very weak sulphur water.

Or take the line to Toulouse, through Auvergne, a much more picturesque route with splendid scenery; the same fare, but a little longer journey. From London, £6 16s. 6d.

The Waters.—They are sodio-sulphuretted warm springs, there being over fifty of them, quite strong in sulphur and iron. These waters are drank, inhaled, sprayed and gargled, as at the other sulphur stations, but here they have a special form of application called *humage*, which consists of the patients sitting around an opening leading to the wells, and directly inspiring the vapours coming from them, through tubes which come from special springs. Having tried this method, we can say that it has decided therapeutic effects.

Therapeutics.— Chronic respiratory affections, scrofula, syphilis, skin-diseases, gun-shot wounds and rheumatism.

Luchon, called Bagnères de Luchon, near the little River Pique, is in one of the most magnificent valleys of the Pyrénées, and is often called the "Queen of the Pyrénées." It certainly is a very beautiful mountain station. The place is also very gay. The casino has public baccara rooms, where ladies are admitted, as at Aix-les-Bains. There are more English and Americans here than at the other stations in this region. The season is from June to September, and the climate is of the bracing order, snow lasting on the rear hills until late in the spring, while storms are frequent in summer. Altitude, 2,000 feet; population, 4,000. Horses abound here, and it is the custom to go riding with a guide to the Vallée du Lys, Lac d'Ao, Grotto du Chat, and even on into Spain, by the routes over Bigorre. It is a fine drive of forty-three miles from here to Bagnères de Bigorre. In walking over the hill under which are the springs, some snakes may be seen; they are not considered harmful.

Physicians.—Dr. Ferras and Dr. Fontan speak English; De Lavarenne, Dr. Kuneman.

Hotels.—Luchon is a dear place and somewhat extravagant town of pleasure, but has good hotels: d'Angleterre, Bonne-Maison, Richelieu, France, Londres, Parc.

SAINT-SAUVEUR (HAUTE PYRÉNÉES).

563 miles from Paris; Orléans R.R. and S. of F. to Pierrefitte; then drive two hours to Saint-Sauveur; twenty-two hours; 100 francs. From London, £7.

Waters.—There are two warm (93° Fah.) sodio-sulphuretted springs of clear water that is soft to the touch, and is well borne by the stomach, owing to the quantity of gas in it. They are considered to be diuretic, tonic and anti-spasmodic.

Therapeutics. — This is the aristocratic French Ladies' Bath, to which nerveless women are sent for all sorts of complaints; diseases of the womb in general, facial neuralgia, sciatica, hysteria and hypochondria. Its therapeutic action has been compared to that of Schlangenbad.

Saint-Sauveur has an altitude of 2,365 feet above sea-level, and seems to be " suspended, as it were, between the Luz Mountains." It is a most picturesque station, but is not as yet frequented by English and American nervous people, notwithstanding its long-standing reputation for such complaints. The Emperor Napoleon III. and Empress Eugénie used to come here. The climate is mild for a mountain region, and while it is somewhat subject to mists, it is considered sedative, and is not so unsettled in summer as some of the Pyrenean stations. There are fine excursions to Luz, Barèges, and on to Cauterets; also to the Pic du Midi, Pic de Bergons, Pic d'Aubiste, Gavarnie, and other high mountain-tops around.

Physicians.—Drs. Blondin, Gaulet, Lafont.

Hotels. — France, Paris, Parc, Bains, Princes. It will be noticed in France that there is always a Hôtel de France, and it is very often one of the oldest and best in the place. Some people live at Luz, which is only a one-mile drive off.*

---

* There are also in the Pyrénées a number of other mineral spring-stations, but they do not have English-speaking customers, and their arrangements are somewhat primitive. We just mention *Saint-Christen, Capvern, Ax, Vernet, Siradan, Encausse, Ussat, Aulus, Olette.*

Saint-Honoré-Les-Bains (Nièvre).

193 miles from Paris, in the centre of France, P.L.M.R.R., to Vandenesse station, then a five mile drive in one and half hours, nine and half hours in all ; 37 francs. From London, £4 16s.

Waters.—There are five springs, giving 220,000 gallons of a clear water, slightly oily and bitter to taste, but with very little smell of sulphur. The temperature is 82° Fah., and the waters have some arsenic in them. In the baths the gas bubbles around the body, and they stimulate the skin. The hot douche to the feet is a special feature here. One enters a room dressed, and taking off shoes and stockings, puts the feet through a hole in the wall, when from the other side a douche of the hot water is played upon them until they are red. This has an excellent derivative action in throat diseases.

Therapeutics. — Chronic throat diseases, skin diseases of a moist type, scrofula, children's diseases, cystitis, metritis, asthma (bronchial form).

Saint-Honoré is the only sulphur water in the centre of France, and has been compared to Eaux Bonnes. It is a pretty little place; population, 1,500; nearly 1,000 feet above sea-level, surrounded by the woods of Morvan. There is the usual casino and music, with charming walks in the woods, and drives to Vielle, or Old Mountain; Château d'Espeuilles, marble quarries, and the iron-works at Fourchambault. The climate is mild.

Physicians.—Drs. Odin (speaks English) and Collin.

Hotels.—Du Morvan, Hardy, Bellevue.

ENGHIEN (SEINE-ET-OISE).

Seven miles from Paris, N. of F.R.R. (Gare du Nord) fifteen minutes from Paris, sixty trains daily, one and half francs. London, £3.

Waters.—These cold, calcareo-sulphated springs, eight in number, are just at the gates of Paris, and contain more actual sulphur than the waters in the far-off Pyrénées. But the latter, naturally hot, contain a substance called Barégine, and Enghien has to heat its waters artificially, which may possibly change their character. Distance, too, lends enchantment, and the mountains possess a great attraction in themselves. At the same time, Enghien is not like many of the dull towns outside of Paris. It is quite a pretty place, with a little lake, and an excellent bathing establishment, with over a hundred baths of all kinds.

Therapeutics.—These waters are useful, being a stimulant, tonic and restorative, with a special action on the skin and mucous membranes of the air passages. They are given for chronic throat and larynx complaints, bronchitis, asthma, skin diseases, heart diseases. Enghien has also established in its bath house electric baths, and the modern treatment by compressed air, as well as rectal injections of sulphuretted compounds. In fact, they claim, according to the microbra theory, that the products derived from the waters are efficient therapeutical agents.

Enghien, called Enghien-les-Bains, is a small town of 2,000 inhabitants, which is agreeable in summer, spring and autumn. Owing to its low altitude (150 feet), and its lake, it is rather damp and cold in winter. Being in the vicinity of Paris, there are crowds of rough pleasure seekers on Sundays, but it is otherwise a good, healthy, summer residence. There are excellent promenades, and excursions to the forest of Montmorency, the Hermitage, &c. There is a pretty little casino, with balls; regattas on the lake, and boating.

Physicians. — Drs. Japhet, Weill. The Paris doctors are also consulted for these waters.

Hotels. — Paix, Quatre Pavillons, Bains, Paris.

PIERREFONDS (OISE).

Sixty miles from Paris, on branch of N.R.R., change at Compiègne. Two hours, 12 francs.

Waters.—This weak sulphur spring is the last of the large class of these waters we shall mention in France. There is also an iron spring at this station, but neither of them

9

has been much used. This is partly owing to the fact that they are too near Paris. It is rather curious that people will prefer to go some distance for their mineral springs. Certainly those near large cities are often neglected. The waters here are cold and not strong, it is true. The bath establishment is a good one, though small, and the station has interest to medical men, for here Dr. Sales Girons invented the spray system of using mineral waters, since adapted for drugs.

Therapeutics.—Throat and bronchial diseases, as usual at sulphur stations, are the principal troubles treated here. Also herpetic skin affections, anæmia and chlorosis, with women's diseases.

Pierrefonds has now direct railway communication. It is a very small place of 1,200 inhabitants, in the great forest of Compiègne. It is celebrated for its beautiful château-fort, called Château de Pierrefonds. It dates from 1390, and is a splendid specimen, perhaps the finest in the world, of an ancient fortified château. It was restored, indeed made new, at great expense, by Viollet le Duc, and is well worth a visit. The Empress Eugénie takes her present title, Countess of Pierrefonds, from this place. Life is very dull here; except for the walks in the splendid forest, there is nothing to do. It has the advantage over Enghien that it is rather farther from Paris, and it does not have a rough Sunday crowd. It has a small casino and reading room, with some music on Sundays.

Physician.—Dr. Janvier.

Hotels.—Du Château, Grand Hotel, Des Ruines.

SALINE SPRINGS.

SALIES DE BÉARN (BASSES PYRÉNÉES).

482 miles from Paris ; Orléans R.R., and S. of F. R.R., to Puyhoo Station ; then a five-mile drive by 'bus or carriage ; sixteen hours ; ninety-six francs. £7 from London.

Waters.—They are brought into one great reservoir in the centre of the village, for use in the manufacture of salt. They are strong, bitter salt waters, sp. gr. 1,208. The so-called "mother water" is the Salies water condensed by evaporation, when it gets brownish in colour, and has a sp. gr. of 1,221. The water being heated night and day, to obtain the salt, sends constant vapours of salt steam into the air, so that the people who stay there are living in a constant salt sea air, without waves or winds. There is a good bathing establishment, and the waters are used internally, as well as mixed with chicken broth. They are soothing, tonic and restorative.

Therapeutics. — Scrofulous children are mostly seen here, with ganglionic and osseous manifestations of that diathesis. Chlorosis and anæmia are treated, as well as rheumatism, paralysis, locomotor ataxy, muscular atrophy and women's diseases.

This little town is at an altitude of 100 feet. Its population is 6,000; it is in a very fine valley in the lower Pyrénées, ten miles from Orthez. The life is quiet. Many people come here from Pau and the adjoining towns, and the French doctors send many patients; but the English and Americans do not frequent the French salt spas to any great extent. There are a number of other salt springs, such as *Salins-Moutiers*, near *Brides*, *Balaruc* and *Bourbon* in the centre of France.

Physicians. — Drs. Musgrave-Clay (English, from Pau,) and Dupeyron.

Hotels. — France, Cheval Blanc, Paris, Bains.

Salins (Jura).

250 miles from Paris; P.L.M.R.R., viâ Dijon; ten hours; forty-eight francs. From London, £5.

Waters. — There are a number of salt springs here, only one of which is reserved for patients, the rest being employed for the salt manufacturers. A visit to the works is interesting and curious. The spring used for patients gives over four millions of gallons per day, of a clear, salt water that is digestive, tonic and resolutive. In large doses it is laxative. The baths are quite complete; one for swimming contains as much as 20,000 gallons that is constantly renewed.

Therapeutics.—The lymphatic constitution; scrofula, necrosis, and caries, white swellings and other tubercular troubles, and Potts's disease. These waters are considered better than sea-baths; they are taken internally as well.

Salins is quite a large town on the River Furieuse; altitude, 1,200 feet; population,

7,000. It is between the mountains of Belies and Saint-André, each of which is crowned with a large fort, making most picturesque and interesting views. A stay here is pleasant. There is the inevitable casino with the usual music. The excursions to Devil's Bridge, Grotto des Planches, Mont Poupet and Bout du Monde, or End of the World, are very interesting. There are good walks in the fine pine woods that surround the town. The climate is warm and rather variable. Season, June to September.

Physicians.—Drs. Guyenot, Bourny.

Hotels.—Bains, Sauvage.

PURGATIVE WATERS.

STRONGLY purgative waters are few in France; they are the only weak point in the "gamut" of the splendid mineral waters of the country.

MONTMIRAIL (VAUCLUSE).

455 miles from Paris, P.L.M.R.R. to Orange; and then, bus in one and half hours; sixteen hours, eighty-two francs. From London, £6.

Waters.—The French physicians, mostly from patriotic motives, give this weak purgative water in place of the other foreign purgative waters, in bottles. They rarely send anyone to the springs, and when it is found that it often takes a whole quart to produce an effect, its use is not continued. It contains sulphates of magnesia and soda.

Therapeutics. — Constipation, abdominal congestion, liver and spleen troubles, women's diseases. Used also after intermittent fevers.

Montmirail is a small village in the southern part of France, near Orange, and has a sulphur and iron spring which is used by people in the vicinity. There is a good establishment.

Physician.—Dr. Millet.
Hotel.—Bains.

Châtel Guyon (Puy De Dôme).

233 miles from Paris, P.L.M.R.R. (Bourbonnais line to Riom) in twelve hours; forty-six francs. From London, £4 16s. 6d., then forty minutes' drive to C.G.

Waters.—They have been compared to Kissingen waters, but their purgative action is due to chlorides, and not to sulphates. They have a saltish taste, and contain gas. They are laxative, exciting to the digestion, and tonic at the same time.

Therapeutics. — They are successful in atony of the intestines, so common in nervous complaints and in approaching age, so that French doctors, as Professor Charcot, send such patients here.

Therapeutics.—Dyspepsia, biliary calculi, gravel, cerebral congestion.

Châtel-Guyon is in the Auvergne district, four miles from Riom, and has an altitude of 1,300 feet.   It is on a little stream called Sardon.

Physician.—Dr. Baraduc.

ALKALINE AND INDIFFERENT SPRINGS.

MONT-DORE (PUY DE DÔME).

289 miles from Paris, P.L.M., or Orléans line to Laqueuille; then 'bus or carriage-drive in one and half hours; twelve hours; fifty-eight francs. From London, £5 4s.

Waters.—There are eight springs at Mont-Dore, all hot, 108° to 110° Fah., giving over 80,000 gallons a day of a feebly mineralized water, without smell or taste, which resembles Neuenahr in Germany. They are sodio-bi-carbonated springs with a small quantity of arsenic in them. They are an example of weak waters, well applied to treatment.

Therapeutics.—These are based on the heat of the water, mostly used in baths and inhaled as hot vapour, and also on drinking the hot water. Stimulation of the skin and perspiration is aimed at here, which seems to end in a sedative action that differs from that of the sulphur springs. In one word, it is a "sweat-box." Chronic affections of respiratory organs, asthma, bronchitis, rheumatic affections, skin diseases, neuralgia, sciatica, are all treated here.

Contra-indications.—All heart troubles and tendency to hæmorrhage must not be sent here.

Mont-Dore has an altitude of 3,400 feet, but population, 2,000. It is a high mountain resort, having a variable climate, with cold mornings and evenings even in summer. The place is comfortable only in July and August. The village is in a narrow valley on the Dordogne, a small stream, and at the base of Angle Mountain, and is a most curious part of old Auvergne. The place is much frequented by priests and clergymen, and the actor and artist class. The walks are high mountain ones, and very beautiful. Excursions to Pic de Sancy, 6,000 feet, to the Cascades de Mont-Dore, La Roche Savadore, and La Bourboule, are recommended.

Physicians. — Drs. Chabory, Edmond (speaks English), Joel, Cazalis, Nicolas.

Hotels.—They are rather dear and not very good. Grand Hotel, Chabory, Mont-joli, Paris, France.

Bookseller.—J. Armet. (See Dobell, "The Mont-Dore Cure.")

ROYAT (PUY DE DÔME).

261 miles from Paris, viâ P.L.M.R.R., Bourbonnais line direct in nine hours ; thirty-four francs. From London, £4 18s.

Waters.—These sodio-bicarbonated, ferruginous arsenical springs contain lithia and a good deal of carbonic acid gas, making a most agreeable soda-water drink. There are four sources and two other springs outside of the company's park, one called *Fonteix*, and another farther out, called *Goudronneuse*. These waters are taken internally, inhaled, gargled, and bathed in. The bathing establishment is a fine one, and the excellent baths have a system of constant renewal of the water while in the bath, that we do not remember to have seen in any other station except in the large piscines or swimming baths. The temperature of the springs varies from 68° to 98° Fah. This place is compared to Ems, but possesses a much better climate, and the scenery is exquisite.

Therapeutics.—The diseases treated are anæmia and chlorosis; all the respiratory troubles of a chronic nature; catarrhs, bronchitis, emphysema, humid asthma. It is also an important station for gout and all gouty affections, gravel, nervous diseases, women's complaints, dyspepsia and diabetes.

Contra-indications.—Acute diseases; cancer, aneurism, and phthisis in acute stage. These contra-indications are much the same for all mineral waters.

After-cures.—The seaside for a short time, except in cases of gout. The bronchial cases would do well to winter in the south of France.

Royat-les-Bains is only fifteen minutes from the large town of Clermont-Ferrand. The altitude is 1,380; population, 2,000. It is as charming a place as any other in Eu-

rope.   The season is end of May to October.
It lies in a valley called Saint-Mart, surrounded by the lower Auvergne Mountains,
which are here well wooded and green.   The
whole country about is pretty.   There are
plenty of fruit-trees, and walnuts and ches-
nuts in abundance.   As to the climate, it is
well open to the west, and sheltered from the
north by the Dôme Mountains ; so that it
has not the variable climate of the higher
Auvergne resorts.   It is a gay little place,
having many visitors—from five to six thousand per year, and two casinos with good
bands of music, concerts, balls and theatrical
performances, and a medical gymnasium.
The excursions to Puy de Dôme and many
other places are very fine.   Notice the old
Roman baths here.   The sanitation is very
good ; the place has never had an epidemic
of any kind.   There is an English church,
lately built.

Physicians.—Drs. G. H. Brandt (is English), Frédet, A. Petit (F.).

Bookseller. — Ribon - Collay.   (See Dr.
Brandt's work on Royat [in English], Dr.

Petit's and Dr. Boucoumont's on the Springs of Auvergne).

Hotels.—The hotels are good, and less expensive than at the more elevated places in this region. Hotels—Continental, Grand Hotel, Européen, Lyon, and many others.

Excursions to the Puy de Dôme, from the summit of which there is a magnificent view. The whole surrounding country is charming.

La Bourboule (Puy de Dôme).

295 miles from Paris by Orléans R.R. to Laqueuille, thence by coach in one hour; eleven hours in all; fifty-five francs. £5 4s. from London.

Waters. — Muriated alkaline arsenical springs, 140° Fah. ; enjoyed a local reputation from very early times. One of the springs long known as the " Source des Fièvres," was brought into prominent notice by the discovery in it of arsenic in 1857. These are the richest hot arsenical waters known. There were six springs, but they are now all united into one, called the

" Choussy - Perrière," giving 9,430 hecto-litres per twenty-four hours. It is a limpid fluid with a salt taste and no smell, used in baths, douches, inhalations, sprays. It contains twenty-eight milligrammes of arsenic per quart of water, which is the equivalent of about twenty-one drops of Fowler's solution, and three grains of sodium chloride and alkaline bicarbonates. In a new sparkling spring lately discovered here there is iron and arsenic, with considerable carbonic acid gas.

Therapeutics.—Lymphatism, struma, scrofula, glandular enlargements, nasal catarrhs, ozæna, lupus, eczema, psoriasis, acne, urticaria and other skin diseases, syphilitic anæmia, chlorosis, intermittent and malarial affections in the chronic stage, diabetes, respiratory troubles, gout, rheumatic dyscrasia and certain cases of arthritis deformans.

La Bourboule, on the Dordogne, altitude 2,700 feet, is in a valley that is extensive and open, while protected north by the mountains, and south it is sufficiently exposed to give it a tonic, sunny and invigorating climate. It

10

has, besides, the charm of that scenery for which Auvergne is justly celebrated. The whole of this district, like other mountain places, is subject to thunderstorms, but they do not last long. The scenery is varied and interesting. The Pic de Sancy rises to a considerable height close by, and on a fine day gives an extensive view as far as the Savoy Alps. With a splendid panorama of the lakes and mountains around, in which the excursions are numerous, the enterprising tourist, artist, geologist, or lover of archæology will find much to interest him here.

The population is 1,500, and number of visitors 10,000. Fine casinos, theatre, English and French Protestant service. Season 25th May to 30th September.

Physicians.—Dr. A. W. Gilchrist (English), Dr. Bertrand, Nicolas and Veyrières.

Hotels.—Des Iles Britaniques, Paris, Ferryroles, Continental, Beau-Sejour. Many furnished apartments. In July and August write in advance for rooms.

Books.—See Dr. Gilchrist's new work in English on the waters.

Néris (Allier).

208 miles from Paris, Orléans line to Montluçon, thence three miles drive to Néris. Fast trains in summer in twelve hours ; forty francs. £4 12s. from London, or to Chamblet station and drive in ten minutes.

Waters.—There are six springs of sodio-chlorinated water, at 115° to 126°. As much as 242,000 gallons of clear water is given per day by these springs. It has no smell, but a slight salt taste. It is mostly used in baths, the establishment being a very complete one with four large swimming baths, douches, vapour baths, &c. It resembles Teplitz in action.

Therapeutics.—The great speciality here is nervous diseases. When rheumatism is allied to the nervous state the French professors send their patients here for neuralgia, sciatica, chorea, hysteria, and all affections allied with a neurotic condition.

Néris is a quiet little village, just what is needed for the kind of patients that come to it ; at the same time it is a pretty place with a little casino and music, and some delightful walks in the park and the woods around. Altitude 800 feet. Population, 2,000. Climate rather hot in summer. Season, May to October. Excursions to Château de l'Ours, Commentry, and Montluçon.

Physicians.—Drs. De Rause, De Grand-maison.

Hotels.—Are good and reasonable. Ten francs is the average charge per day. Paris, France, Dumoulin, Europe, Rome.

VICHY (ALLIER).

228 miles from Paris, P.L.M.R.R. (Bourbonnais line), direct in eight hours, forty-one francs. From London, £4 12s. 10d.

Waters.—They are the type of soda waters, or sodio-bicarbonated. Hot and cold springs, fifteen regular wells and a number in the neighbourhood, at Cusset, and in the town itself. Some of them are pure alkaline waters, others contain more iron. They are used for drinking and baths mostly. The establishment here is under the Government, and is a very fine one. Indeed, there are three or four large bathing establishments containing all the modern hydropathic appliances. The water is clear, or but slightly troubled in the hot springs. The taste of the Grande Grille is not disagreeable to most people. Used in bottles it should be drank according to physician's orders. The wells differ considerably, and according to the complaint, it makes quite a difference what kind of Vichy one uses, although they are all bicarbonated waters. The Source l'Hôpital is for hepatic disorders, also the Grande Grille; the "Celestins" is for the gout; the "Lardy" contains much iron, and so on.

Therapeutics.—Stomach complaints in general, dyspepsia, liver, spleen and bladder troubles, gout, catarrh of uterus and diabetes, stone, Bright's disease, malarial cachexia, anæmia (Mesdames spring).

Vichy is the most thronged mineral spring in France, if not in the world, nearly fifty thousand visitors going there in the season. It is open all the year, but frequented like most places in summer—May to October.

It is in a valley on the river Allier, in the great central plains before reaching the mountains of Auvergne, at an altitude of 780 feet ; population, 6,000. The climate is hot and relaxing in summer, while the place itself is not in the best sanitary condition. The river is usually very low, almost dry in fact, and the immediate country around is not at all interesting. A drive, however, of a few miles brings one to some sub-Alpine scenery in the Forey mountains. In Vichy itself there is a good park and a central garden, in which is the largest bath establishment in France, and at the other end a fine casino or club room with splendid theatre where all the best Paris artists perform during the season, and a reading room with card rooms provided. There are balls, concerts, and excellent music.

Physicians.—Dr. Cormack (English), Villemin, Audhair, and one hundred others (F.).

Bookseller.—M. Cæsar. See Dr. Cormack's large work in English on Vichy waters.

Hotels.—Ambassadeurs, Parc, Grand, Victoria, Cherbourg, Princes, Paix, Nouvel Hôtel.

POUGUES (NIÈVRE).

150 miles from Paris, on P.L.M., Bourbonnais line, direct in four hours, twenty-nine francs. From London £4 1s.

Waters.—This is a cold calcaro-bicarbonated spring called St. Leger, used mostly for drinking, and it is a most excellent table water, but it possesses qualities that make it much recommended in certain diseases. It is diuretic, aperient, and tonic. There is a small bathing establishment, but the waters are mostly used for drinking purposes. They are sent out bottled in large quantities. There is a second spring used in baths.

Therapeutics.—Dyspepsia, gravel, certain forms of albuminuria and other nephritic troubles of a chronic nature, anæmia and chlorosis, as there is much iron in the water, and women's diseases are also treated.

Pougues-les-Eaux is a small village eight miles from the large city of Nevers. It is healthy, lying in the great central plain of

France near the Loire, at 700 feet altitude; population, 1,500. The climate is warm in summer, but steady; there are none of the storms of the mountains. Season, May to October. It is extremely quiet at Pougues, but there is some music, and there are nice walks in the neighbourhood. The celebrated china manufactories at Nevers are worth a visit.

Physicians.—Dr. Janicot (speaks English), and Dr. Bovet.

Hotels are few in number, rather dear and not good. There being no market all has to be brought from Nevers. Hôtel Splendide, Parc, France.

DAX (LANDES).

458 miles from Paris, Orléans R.R. and S. of F. direct. Fifteen hours, eighty-one francs. From London, £6 4s. Main line Paris to Madrid.

Waters.—There is an immense spring of hot alkaline water, some ten yards square from which vapour arises that in certain seasons can be seen for miles around. Besides this, the river overflows its banks, and the mud is collected and used for baths. The water is weak, and flows over 500,000 gallons per day. It is used not as a drink, but simply as baths and with the mud. It has no taste or smell. Patients here reside in the establishments, and the water is supplied to them there.

Therapeutics.—Dax is the place for the worst cases of joint trouble, anchylosis, rheumatism, gout, neuralgia, gun-shot wounds, hysteria, early phthisis. The mineral mud baths are the great feature.

Dax is open all the year round. In winter the principal hotel has glass galleries, 800 feet around the passages, and has its rooms very nicely warmed. The town is in the midst of the great pine forests which stretch from Arcachon to Biarritz. It is also close to Pau, so that its claim to being a winter station is as good, if not better, than Pau. Mean temperature in winter, 48° Fah. ; altitude, 130 feet.

It is quite a large town—10,000 population, with paved streets ; but it is very dull, and the sanitary condition is not good. The life here is indoor in winter, and in summer there are some good drives in the pine forest with fishing along the river.

Physicians. — Dr. Barthe de Sandfort (speaks English), and Dr. Lerema.

Hotels.—The principal ones are the Thermes, Europe, France.

CONTREXÉVILLE (VOSGES).

233 miles from Paris. E. of F. R.R. direct in nine hours, forty-one francs. From London, £4 10s.

Waters.—There are four cold calcaro-bicarbonated springs (55° F.), with a fresh taste and after-taste styptic. The great value of the water is in its diuretic action. The kidneys eliminate it rapidly, and the urine secretion is stimulated. Baths and douches are used, but drinking the water is the important treatment. They are slightly laxative.

Therapeutics.—Kidney complaints, vesical catarrh, inertia and paralysis of bladder, retention and incontinence of urine, prostatic enargements, chronic cystitis, gravel, diabetes.

Contrexéville is 1,000 feet above sea level on the river Vair, in the Vosges mountains, in the North-east of France, on R.R. to Nancy, the line of the Orient Express. The climate is slightly variable, but not so cold in the mornings and evenings as other mountain resorts. Population, 1,000. There is the usual casino and music, theatres, &c., with a fine park for walking as well as excellent drives in the hills around the town. Season, June to September.

Physicians. — Drs. Debout d'Estrées, Boursier, Graux, Boichoux.

Hotels.—Etablissement, Mabboux, Paris, Providence.

VITTEL (VOSGES).

This is the next station to Contrexéville on same R.R.

Waters.—The Grand Spring is claimed to be as good as Contrexéville, and the salt spring better. In respect to iron it would seem that these waters contain more than the last mentioned springs. A still stronger iron spring here is called the "Source des Demoiselles."

Therapeutics.—Grande Spring-Gravel and diseases of urinary passages.

Salt Spring.—Biliary calculi, congestion of liver, constipation, &c. Anæmia is treated by the iron spring mentioned above.

Vittel is one of the Vosges mountain places on the Vair and three miles only from Contrexéville. Population, 1,500. Altitude, 1,100 feet. It is a picturesque healthy place now much frequented. There are the usual public sitting rooms, and the establishment is on high ground above the village. There are good horses and carriages, and the excursions in these hills are noted as very good indeed.*

Physicians.—Drs. Bouloumié, Rodet (both speak English).

Books.—Dr. Rodet, "English Guide to Vittel."

Hotels.—Etablissement, Commerce, Source.

---

* *Martigny-les-Bains* is in this district of France.

PLOMBIÈRES (VOSGES).

251 miles from Paris, E. of R.R., ten hours, fifty francs.

Twenty-eight springs. These hot and cold waters are clear and tasteless, and slightly oily to the feel. They are called "Simple Indeterminate Waters" by the French, yet the establishment is one of the largest in France, and the number of visitors is very large. We have before called attention to the fact that the feebly-mineralised waters are more frequented than the strong ones. People go to Aix, Mont Dore, &c., and but little to very strong springs like Challes, for instance. This is largely owing to the method of application of the waters rather than to the mineral elements in them. The mechanical treatment under water and massage are given. Plombières is compared to Teplitz.

Therapeutics.—This is quite a ladies' station. Irregularities in menstruation, uterine complaints, sterility, leucorrhœa, gastro-intestinal troubles and nervous diseases, lumbago, while anæmia is treated by the Iron Spring, "La Bourdeille."

Rheumatism is also treated by the hot waters, which range from 70° to 160° Fah.

Contra-indication.—Phthisis.

Plombières (pronounced Plum-be-air) is in a very deep narrow valley on the Augronne, a torrent, and something like Spa, in Belgium, it lies so low that it is not seen until you are quite close to it. It is, however, 1,360 feet above the sea level. The population is 2,000. The climate is healthy; although hot in summer there are storms enough to keep the evenings and mornings cool. There is a fine casino, and on the Promenade des Dames life is not wanting during the season. There are also delightful excursions in the neighbouring mountains, to the old ruined Abbey of Revirmont, the valley of Semouze, &c.*

Physicians. — Drs. Bottentuit, Malibran, Liétard.

Hotels.—Grand Hôtel, Tête d'Ôr, Lion d'Ôr.

---

* The *Bussang* Iron Spring is near here, but is not much frequented. It is, however, a most charmingly

Evian-les-Bains (Haute-Savoie).

This station is on the French side of *Lake of Geneva* (called Lake Leman). It can be reached by boat from Geneva in four hours or in half-an-hour by steamer from Lausanne, Switzerland, almost opposite. (Two francs). *Lausanne* is 330 miles from Paris in eleven hours, sixty francs, P.L.M.R.R. From London, £5 8s. 3d.

Waters. — There are five very slightly mineralised springs at Evian. They are cold, calcareo-bicarbonated waters; it is a splendid table water, clear and agreeable to drink. Their properties are diuretic and tonic. The first is the most important. They are given in large quantities, to wash out, as it were, the bladder as well as the blood and eliminate the uric acid. They are considered a good after-cure to follow Aix-les-Bains.

Therapeutics.—Catarrhal affections of the

---

situated place in the heart of the Vosges mountains, and very attractive for those who desire a quiet retreat. Chronic diarrhœas and anæmia are cured here. The water is very largely exported.

bladder form the great speciality of this station. Gravel, irritability of the urinary organs, dyspepsia, gastralgia and stomach complaints, and gout, are treated here.

Evian is a pretty little town, population 3,000, . on south side of the lake, almost opposite to Lausanne, and twenty-five miles from Geneva, but in France. Altitude, 1,350 feet ; mild, pleasant tonic climate, with rather strong winds at times from the lake. It is much frequented in summer. There is a casino with plenty of music. The excursions are numerous. One can run over to Lausanne, Vevey, and in fact to all the pleasure places on the lake, both Swiss and French sides. In the neighbourhood of Evian are the Château de Neucelles, the ruins of the Château de Maxilly, and the Grotto of Jean Jacques Rousseau.

Physicians.—Drs. Roques, Taberlet, Million.

Hotels.—Grand Hôtel des Bains, Hôtel France, Paix, Alpes.

Amphion (Savoy).

This station is only twenty minutes out from Evian ; two miles by tramway.

Waters. — They are weak, bicarbonated and ferruginous cold springs, containing a certain quantity of ·oxide of iron. The quantity of water is very large, and they are used for baths also.

Therapeutics. — Anæmia and chlorosis. The waters are also used as at Evian, and for the same diseases, but the great advantage of this place is its adaptability as an after cure for Aix-les-Bains and other stations where more serious cures are carried out.

Amphion-les-Bains is a cheerful summer residence, and has one of the best views in Europe. From the top of a hill back of the place, looking over all the Lake of Geneva, can be seen the grandest and most varied of panoramas. In fine weather it is one of the loveliest spots in Europe. The Jura Mountains are behind it. The steamers ply regularly and frequently on the lake to Lausanne, Montreux, &c. As the place was at one time

11

a gambling station, like Monte Carlo, no expense was spared in laying out the grounds. Fishing is good here. Altitude, 1,350 feet. It is windy at times (like Evian), from the " Bise," or N.E. winds.

Physician.—Dr. Dumur.

Hotels. — Grand Hôtel d'Amphion, Des Bains.

Other Ferruginous French Springs.—The pure iron waters are not numerous in this country, but nearly all of its mineral waters contain some iron, while the Corsican waters of *Orezza* and *Pardina* are very strong iron waters. Besides these we have *La Bauche* in Savoy, which is but little frequented. A good iron water not yet much known is *Renlaigue*. *Orezza* and *Pardina*, bottled, are much used in France.

RENLAIGUE (PUY DE DÔME).

This is in the south-west part of this department and not as yet much known, but as its great merits will certainly bring it soon into notice, we mention it. The water contains a large quantity of carbonic acid gas making it very digestible and agreeable.

Forges les Eaux (Seine Inférieure).

Seventy - three miles from Paris. West of F.R.R. ; three and a-half hours ; fifteen francs.

These are cold, pure ferruginous springs. There are three of them in the private establishment, which is small and not well-arranged ; and there is an open free spring in the fields beyond, which is believed to be just as good. The waters all taste like ink, and contain very little, if any, gases.

Therapeutics.—Anæmia, chlorosis, amenorrhœa, hysteria, and all cases of general weakness and convalescence from disease, when iron can be borne.

Forges is in the fertile valley of Bray, and the smiling country of Normandy, with its fine cows, butter and milk in abundance. But in contra - distinction to the country around, the town itself is dull and dirty. There is a small room used as a casino, but nothing of the amusement that is to be found at other watering places ; so that this station is only for serious invalids, who can stand its inconveniences and expense for the benefit of the excellent iron water. Try the Normandy cider here. The climate is mild and rainy.

Physicians.—Drs. Cavé, Mathon.

Hotels.—Des Thermes, Mouton. (The hotels are poor and dear at this station.)*

---

* There is a spring near Paris called *Forges-les-Bains,* with weak iron waters, very little used.

FRENCH SEASIDE AND SUMMER CLIMATIC AIR STATIONS.

WE mention first the fact that nearly all the mineral water stations are Climatic Air Stations *for summer*, owing to their situation in high mountain valleys. The French sea coast is a very long one, stretching as it does all the way from Dunkerque and Calais on the English Channel to the Atlantic by Arcachon and Biarritz, on again to the Mediterranean and along its coast from Marseilles to Mentone. The most frequented places are *Dieppe, Boulogne sur Mer, Étretat, Trouville, St. Malo, Houlgate, Dinard, Dinan, Concarneau, Royan, Arcachon, Biarritz,* and *St. Jean de Luz.* The Mediterranean stations, *Cannes, Nice,* and *Mentone,* while they possess bathing apparatus, are used mostly by the natives, although there is no question but what the famous inland sea has more salt in it than the Atlantic, so that the baths should be of great value. But fashion has decreed otherwise and the world blindly follows it, and goes to the Atlantic sea-side resorts. The temperature is never excessive on the great tideless sea. Still it must be admitted that it is colder at the seaside in the North, and there are no breakers in the southern sea.

In regard to summer holidays at sea, notwithstanding the advances that have been made the last ten years in building great steamers and providing for the welfare of passengers by them, so great are the evils of ocean travel, even first-class, that but few invalids are nowadays advised to go down to the great deep for health. It must, however, be said that more discomfort and sea-sickness may be experienced in crossing from Dover to Calais in bad weather than in a trip around the world in a large well-arranged steamer. A sea voyage can be recommended to many middle-aged business men who break down, and to others who need to escape letters and telegrams and the weary treadmill of business for a time. The over-energetic American put on board ship, where he cannot do anything more energetic than walk the deck, and where he no longer gets his morning paper, is forced to rest.

Sea-bathing itself is best adapted for delicate women and girls, and also for children and over-worked men. It improves the general health and braces the system against catching cold, and it is a tonic to the cerebro-spinal system. We must make special mention of its effects on scrofulous children. The contra-indications are eye diseases, and some of the skin diseases as well as chorea and convulsive troubles of any kind. Sufferers from diseases of the heart and lungs, gout, with any tendency to cerebral congestion, as well as highly irritable and nervous people, had better not use sea-baths. Mountain air would be best for these cases. We mention a few of the most popular sea-baths.

Therapeutics of Sea-Baths. — As above, muscular debility and exhaustion, tuberculosis in joints, white swellings, &c. They help those who need repose and convalescents.

BOULOGNE SUR MER (PAS DE CALAIS).

159 miles from Paris, northern line, five hours; twenty-nine francs. From London, £1 12s.

This well-known port and watering-place on the Channel hardly needs description. It was for a long time the resort, all the year round, of many English people who found it convenient to be near England and yet away from it, but at present there are not so many English residents as there were; 2,000 is the estimated number. In summer this number is greatly increased. The quay is over 5,000 feet long. The sea-bathing is fair, sands excellent. Population, 50,000; innumerable smells, a splendid casino. Season, July to August.

Physicians.—Drs. Bourgain, Gros, Patin.

Bookseller.—Merridew's English Library.

There are several English clubs, the United, Cricket, and the Lawn Tennis club.*

---

* On this coast is *Berck sur Mer* which has a celebrated Marine Hospital for scrofulous and tubercular children, that has had such wonderful success

DIEPPE (SEINE INFÉRIEURE).

104 miles from Paris, Western R.R., in four hours ; seventeen francs. From London, £1 4s. 7d.

These much frequented sea-baths are at the mouth of the Argues. The town is a bright, lively one ; population, 22,000. It is the chief fishing station on this coast, and much amusement is got on the pier watching the fishing boats coming and going. The beach itself is a pebble one and not agreeable ; sandals must be worn. The breakers are good, but not so fine as on the more open Atlantic coast. There is a handsome casino with theatre, and considerable gambling, &c. It is often very cold, so that July, or better, August, is recommended for a stay ; then it is full of life and gaiety. As at all watering-places in France, the beach and baths are under the superintendence of a Physician-Inspector.

---

in all chronic enlargements of the cervical and sub-maxillary glands and joints. This hospital has been imitated in places on account of the advances made there in different cures of scrofula.

Physicians.—Drs. Caron, De la Rue, De Parel.

Bookseller. — Rainville, Grande Rue, No. 52.

Hotels.—Royal, Des Bains, Grand, Des Étrangers (all expensive).

TROUVILLE SUR MER (CALVADOS).

137 miles from Paris. People go to Havre by rail, and cross over to Trouville on the sea by a little steamer (ten miles), four hours and a half; nineteen francs.

This is the fashionable sea-side place of France. It has an excellent sandy beach, which is quite flat and safe for children. There is no shingle here, and one can walk for miles on the sands. There are hundreds of pretty villas in the English style with a fine club or casino containing all the usual elements of society; it cost 60,000 dollars. Balls are frequent. The population is 7,000. Season, June to September. The races are very good here in August.

Physicians.—Drs. Legoupil, Leneveu.

Hotels. — Are all very dear. De Paris, Roches Noires, Belle Vue, Plage and others.*

St. Malo (Ille et Vilaine).

Western R.R., six hours; forty-two francs. This old seaport town is much frequented by the French. It is in Brittany, facing Servan and Dinard at the mouth of the Rance. Its ancient ramparts form a good promenade, and the beach is of firm, hard sand. The winter climate is milder than that of England, and is bracing in summer. The mean of January is 41°, of July 69°. Population, 12,000. Steamers from here to the Island of Jersey twice a week.

Physicians.—Drs. Ferrand, Noury.

Hotels.—France, Univers, Franklin.†

Arcachon (Gironde).

400 miles from Paris. Orléans line to Bordeaux, and S. of F. on; twelve hours,

---

* Near by are *Houlgate, Etretat* and *Cabourg*. *Déauville* is connected with Trouville by a bridge.

† *Pornic, Royan* and *Le Croisic* are close by on the west coast, but are thoroughly French seaside places.

seventy-four francs. From London, £5 17s.,
viâ Dover.

Arcachon—population, 5,000 ; in summer
50,000 to 60,000—is thirty-four miles from
Bordeaux, and is reached in an hour from
there. The name of the place means resin,
in the language of the country. This is
owing to the immense pine-forests that ex-
tend on all sides, and give resin. The town
is not on the sea, but on an immense sea
basin many miles in extent, so that the bathing is quiet; but good swimmers like the
place. The place is divided into two distinct parts. The first is the large, long, flat
lower town, three miles long, or "Summer
Town," with thousands of small one and two
storey houses, which are used by the sea-
bathers, who flock here in hundreds of thousands during the summer season for the
excellent swimming, fishing and yachting.
The oyster culture in the immense basin is
a wonderful sight and most interesting ; ten
millions of oysters are sold yearly. It is
possible to go out to the Bay of Biscay
and get real open sea - bathing, and also

sand baths in summer time, but it is five miles off.

We now come to the second side of Arcachon, its " Ville d'Hiver," or winter city. The streets of the town lead up to an immense sand dune in the midst of a pine forest; here are a number of pretty villas and hotels which make up the winter resort. It is a moderately mild soothing climate, suitable to cases of irritative bronchial and laryngeal catarrh, and sufferers from nervous disease who like quiet. It is not at all suitable to persons of torpid or lymphatic nature, and those who need a more stirring life; they do better in the tonic and stimulating air of the Riviera.

The mean winter temperature is 50° some years and 46° others.

There are nearly 9,000 acres of pine woods here, which have a most peculiar stillness, owing to the deep sand roads and walks not giving any sound, and the pine trees having no leaves to rustle. Dr. Fagge, now of Monte Carlo, during two winters at Arcachon, observed only two days of fog and six of frost.   In winter the city is desolate; shops are closed until summer, and there is no gaiety.   The water supply is pretty good, but the drainage indifferent.   The quantity of rain is considerable, but it dries off rapidly in the sand.

Physicians.—Drs. Festal, Hameau, Lalesque.

Hotels.—On the beach, Grand Hôtel, Royal, France; in the pine woods, Hôtel de la Forêt, Hôtel des Pins.

BIARRITZ (BASSES PYRÉNÉES).

Viâ Bordeaux and S. of F.R.R.; sixteen hours, ninety francs from Paris. From London, £6 12s.

This is a fashionable resort, partly Spanish, but frequented by the richer English.   It is on the Bay of Biscay, sixty-eight miles from Bordeaux.   The station called "Negresse" is almost three-quarters of an hour's drive from the town on the beach.   Biarritz is situated on a cliff, and it has no less than three amphitheatres of pretty beaches with splendid breakers rolling in from the Atlantic. In regard to bracing fine sea-bathing there is no place to compete with Biarritz. It is suited to persons of a lethargic constitution. The winds are strong, blowing over its towering cliffs like a fury. It is far enough south to have been recommended as a winter resort, but from the months of December to May it is not suitable to any real invalids, although the climate is bright and exhilarating for a great part of the year. It suits rather strong hysterical and hypochondriacal patients, and those who suffer from depressed states of the nervous system, but no other diseases. Some asthmatics do well here. There is a fine casino with music, &c.; the population is 6,000. There is a tramway now running to Bayonne in three-quarters of an hour, a large place where one can live more reasonably than at Biarritz.

Physicians.—Drs. Malpas and Mackew (English).

Hotels.—These are all dear ; Grand, Angleterre, Victoria, Continental. The Villa du Midi is an English boarding house, but Biarritz is a place for rich people only.

We now come to the south coast of France which will be described among " Winter Resorts." *

---

* *St. Jean de Luz* is twenty minutes by train farther on, close to *Hendaye* and the Spanish frontier, and is a very pretty place with splendid beach on another of the semi-circular bays like Biarritz. The climate is more sheltered, and some English pass the winter here. The sea-bathing is good. There is no boating on this coast, as it is rough and dangerous. Hôtel d'Angleterre, Paris. Dr. Goyenèche.

WINTER RESORTS AND HOMES
FOR INVALIDS IN FRANCE.

It dates back to the highest antiquity that after long and patient observation and study, physicians have recommended delicate patients to pass their winters on the Mediterranean coast. Since it has many times been proved by actual experiment that the western Riviera contains the best winter stations that exist in Europe, we agree with Dr. Yeo who says, " That a perfect climate cannot be found," and after a residence of two years in Egypt, and many seasons passed in the most renowned winter climates, we are confident that the many thousands of English and Americans who pass their winters on the Riviera have the best reasons to believe that they have found the next best to a perfect climate, or at least the nearest possible approach to one.*   The advantages are a sunny atmosphere, a slight rainfall, mostly confined to October ; no snow or fogs, and but little frost, and if any, only in the morning of a few days in the worst months.   It is a dry, tonic air climate ; that is, mild ; but it must not be supposed that the south of France is a tropical climate with all its relaxing elements.   In fact, here as elsewhere, winter will be winter, and one must study the weather to live long, and take certain precautions to get full benefit from the climate (see Dr. Linn on " Precautions for the Climate of Nice ").   Between October and May there are over 100 clear cloudless days on the Riviera ; in London during the same time there are about ten, and nearly a 100 rainy days.   Then there is hardly a single day on which an invalid cannot go out at

---

* The climate of the *Hawaiian Islands* (latitude 20-23 n.), is probably the most perfect in the world, being never either cold, very hot, or windy at the sea-level, where the range of temperature is from 65 to 80 Fah.   On the mountains it is cool according to the elevation.

least for some portion of the day in the
South.   Besides, one is in touch with the
world and civilisation, and within a few hours
of the great cities.   We well remember with
what annoyance we read our six-day-old
paper in Egypt during one rainy day with
hail and cold wind.   To escape the cold and
damp of the North is the reason why all
these thousands come to the South.   Are
they right in doing so?   When so large a
number of human reasoning beings do a
thing they are mostly right in doing it, even
if for no other reason than that which makes
the birds migrate.   We are convinced that
intuition is truth.   It may be true this
modern theory of micro-organisms having
something to do with the cause of pneumonia
and kindred diseases are correct, but certainly the part taken by exposure to cold and
damp is the most important factor in all
chest and bronchial troubles.   This all prac-
tical physicians know by clinical facts, and
this knowledge is worth more than a thousand theories.   Even if the microbes are the
seeds of disease they will not develop on

healthy soil, so to speak, the ground must be prepared to receive them. The manner of this preparation in the human frame is well known. We get overheated in a damp, cold climate, and we catch the disease, how? The mere mechanical effect of the cold contracts the little blood vessels which run just beneath the surface of the skin; this drives the blood away from these parts, and must create a congestion somewhere else—most likely in one of our vital organs, or wherever we have our weak spot, the so-called *locus minoris resistentiæ*, and this point of least resistance is least apt to recover promptly from the congestion produced. The old saying that " warmth is life and cold is death " is true. That cold checks our perspiration, and prevents the carrying off of the injurious, worn-out, and poisonous materials from the body, and throws the work of purification on the internal organs, we all know. The kidneys and lungs may not be in the best condition to perform the skin's function or help it along, and congestion and the maladies follow. It is true that many hundreds of the people who flock south in winter do so for society and amusement, and for many invalids this is an excellent thing. Why should sick people be " cabined, cribbed, confined " in dull villages where they see no life about them, even if they have some comforts? The so-called moral influence is immense in all diseases, from the toothache that goes away at the dentist's door to *maladie imaginaire* that does not come on when we feel that we are in reach of medical skill. Taking hysterical cases alone, we remember the case of an imaginary tumour that came on in the country, and disappeared as soon as it came under the city surgeon's eye. These are some of the advantages of wintering in a mild, dry climate, where every comfort and convenience can be had. The main climatic characteristics of the Riviera are the same at all of the stations, but each has its own secondary qualities. " While all of these winter resorts have the same dry tonic climates, they each have spots that are more or less sheltered than the rest of the town. This is owing to some natural protection given by a hill or a clump of trees behind the quarter of the place in question." It is a matter, therefore, of paramount importance to persons who intend wintering on the Riviera, not only to select the place, but to find out what part of the town is most suitable to them. This can best be done by consulting the local physicians. It is just as injudicious to solve this question by the advice of the inexpert, as it would be to accept medical advice or drugs from anyone who chose to proffer them.

Having considered in a general way the climate of the south we pass on to review the principal resorts, but only from the medical point of view; leaving to regular guide books the description of the sights. We will speak as briefly as possible of the places as far as they are interesting in a health giving way; describing the temperatures, climates, &c., as well as sanitation, and naming leading physicians.

ALGIERS, AFRICA (BELONGS TO FRANCE).

P.L.M.R.R. to Marseilles, then steamer to Algiers, fifty-four hours in all; 145 francs (forty hours' passage). From London, £9 18s.

The climate is said to be slightly warmer and more humid than the resorts on the French Riviera. The number of rainy days in winter is given as eighty-seven, barometric pressure 762 mm.; the mean temperature is 60° Fah. In January and February it rains a good deal, when it does not on the French side; the best months here are considered to be March and April. In regard to nervous complaints the climate is less exciting than Nice for instance. The drainage is not as good as it should be; the old town is very dirty, but most of the new parts are better. The upper part of the town called *Mustapha Superior* is the best portion. The touch of oriental life here is interesting. For those who suffer from sea-sickness there is little in Algiers to compensate their sufferings (Dr. Yeo) in crossing from Marseilles.

Therapeutics.—Protracted recovery from

pleurisy and chest complaints. Early phthisis when the nervous excitability contra-indicates the dry resorts of the Riviera. Dry forms of bronchitis, asthma, Bright's disease.

Contra-indications.—Bilious people should not go to Algiers.

There are amusing paper-chases, hunts, battles of flowers, &c., in Algiers.

Physicians.—Dr. Thompson (English), Dr. Pepper (American).

Hotels.—Hôtel D'Orient, Regence ; Villa Russell, Grand, Kirsch, Des Palmiers, Mrs. Jennings. (The expense is slightly more than in France itself).*

HYÈRES (VAR).

590 miles from Paris, P.L.M.R.R. viâ Marseilles to Toulon or to La Pauline where change for H. Sixteen hours, 105 francs. From London, £7 6s.

---

* *Hamman R'Irha*, fifty miles off, altitude, 2,000 feet, with hot springs, gives an agreeable change from Algiers. The waters are used for rheumatism, &c. *Blida* is another Algerian winter station.

This town of 14,000 population, altitude, 650 feet, is three miles away from the sea, and is often recommended to invalids who cannot bear the more stimulating air of the places on the sea-coast itself. It, however, is the least sheltered and is exposed to the mistral winds. It claims notwithstanding to be more soothing or at least less exciting than the other resorts, while the air is not so dry. This constitutes the advantage of Hyères in certain cases. It is only thirteen miles distant from the important city and port of Toulon. Life is very quiet at this station, but it has a greater variety of drives and walks than Mentone and many of the other towns, as Monte Carlo, &c. The old part consists of steep, narrow streets running up the castle hill. It has, however, its new quarter with handsome new streets and villas, where the elevation is seventy feet above the plain. Snow falls rarely and does not last; sixty rainy days is the average; winter temperature rarely below 43° Fah. The drainage has been improved.

Therapeutics.—Rheumatism, nervous and

feeble children, and adults, Bright's disease, scrofula. The question of the suitability of this place for phthisis and the respiratory troubles is a much disputed one and must be decided according to the case. 4,000 families stay here over winter, and 80,000 visitors come from October to May. Fifty-six fine days in winter.*

Contra-indications.—It is not considered favourable for many cases of asthma.

Physicians. — Drs. Biden and Cormack (English), Bourgarel (French).

Hotels.—Continental, Albion, Parc, Palmiers, Iles d'Or, Europe.

Bookseller.—T. Hébrard.

CANNES (ALPES MARITIMES).

660 miles from Paris, 120 from Marseilles, and nineteen from Nice. P.L.M.R.R. direct in eighteen and half hours ; 119 francs. From London, £7 15s. 3d.

---

* *Castabelle*, about two miles south-west of the Hyères has some good villas and new hotels in pine woods. The number of its visitors is increasing rapidly, the Queen of England having been there in March, 1892.

The mean temperature is 50° Fah., ten degrees higher than London. In winter it rarely falls below 51° from ten to six. There are fifty-eight rainy days. Near the sea the air is tonic and stimulant; while at Cannet, inland, as inland in California, the climate is quite different. Cannes is open and windy like the rest of this coast, when it is not closely protected by the hills. The screen of mountains here is only moderately high. In one word the town climate is bracing in winter, and mild and agreeable in spring. The altitude is fifty feet; 10,000 strangers settle here in winter, and fifty or sixty thousand pass through the town. The population is 20,000.

Therapeutics.—Anæmia, chlorosis, catarrhal affec ons, phthisis, laryngitis, bronchial complaints, rheumatism, gout, diabetes, age and general weakness, Bright's disesase, phthisis, scrofula. (The last shoul' be treated close to the sea-side). Asthma and emphysema do well on the more elevated parts.

Life at Cannes is of the quiet order. There are not many amusements, the theatre only being open when the managers at Nice send over a partial company. There is a new casino however, and some good clubs, and once one is acquainted in society there is plenty of visiting to do. The walks are good, as it only takes a few minutes to get out into the country. The town is free from noise or excitement. There are many fine villas at Cannes, and large streets are laid out, but these are overbuilt, and as yet not fully occupied.

English Churches.—Three of them, and a Scotch church.

Physicians.—Drs. Bright, Blanc, Frank, Duke, Agnes Maclaren (English), and De Valcourt (F.).

Dentists.—Hurlburt, Doremus (Americans).

Hotels.—Pavillion, Princes, Grand, Bellevue, Anglais, Metropole, Continental, Gray et Albion, Paradis, Beausite.

Bookseller.—Robaudy, Rue d'Antibes. English reading room, No. 45, Rue de Fréjus. See Dr. Blanc's "Advice to Intending Visitors to Cannes."

GRASSE.

This little village is about eleven miles north of Cannes, 1,050 feet altitude. The train on the branch line takes forty minutes to mount the inclined road which leaves the main P.L.M.R.R. at La Bocca. There is now a railway direct from Nice to Grasse, S.R.R. The natural situation is one of great picturesqueness, standing high upon the hillside. The village commands a view over all the country extending to the sea.

It has some advantages over Cannes in the matter of climate, being much better protected from wind. The altitude also gives purer and more sedative air ; on the other hand, it is a cooler place th n its neighbours. It is beneficial to sufferers from asthma and gout, to nervous invalids, and for insomnia, rheumatism, neuralgia, &c. The sanitary co .dition is far from perfect, but the water supply is good. A system of modern drainage is under consideration. The excursions in these hills are very fine. The Queen of England passed one winter at Grasse (1891).

Hotels.—Grand Hôtel, Victoria.

Physicians. — Drs. Chabert, Laugier (French).

NICE (ALPES MARITIMES).

630 miles from Paris, P.L.M.R.R. ; 140 miles from Marseilles (Lyons station), direct by the new trains in nineteen hours; 122 francs. From London, £7 18s.

Climate of Nice.—There is great difficulty in making people understand that the south of France, in December, January and February, is not a *tropical* climate. It is not so ; it is simply one in which the cold of the north is tempered, and rendered less severe, by the sun. It is always warmer than the north, and has a great number of sunny days, when invalids can carry out the great object of climatic treatment, viz., *the spending of as much time as possible in the open air.*

Nice (pronounced *Neece*) is in latitude N. 43° 41′ 39″ and 4° 55′ 22″ longitude E. It has nearly 90,000 inhabitants and about 60,000 more during the winter. About a million of people visit the city every year.

It may be called the capital city of winter health resorts. It is the only city on the Riviera, the rest being towns. *Cannes*, with 20,000 population, is the next largest, but no comparison is possible. The city lies in a circle between the hill of *Villefranche*, which protects it from the east winds, and the promontory called Cap d'Antibes, which keeps off partly the strong mistral wind, of which much is said in works on the Midi. This wind is a north-north-west one ; the peasants call it " the good wind," and to anyone in fair health it has nothing unpleasant about it. The local opinion is that it blows away much that may do harm in the town. The sirocco is the south or south-south-east wind, supposed to come from the African deserts, and it is rare at Nice. The mean atmospheric pressure is 761 mm. Dryness is the chief characteristic of the climate. It is a tonic, exciting atmosphere. From October to May there are 135 sunny days. The mean annual temperature is $59\frac{1}{2}°$ Fah. These climatic figures vary as they do everywhere, and can only be general in statement. We have our mild and bad winters here as elsewhere, but *there* are often winters when the thermometer will not fall below 46° Fah. On the rare occasions when frost occurs it is invariably at night, and the bright morning sun makes short work of it. Some years it actually snows a little in Nice itself, but it only remains a few hours on the ground, and this has never been more than part of one day in any year. Fogs are unknown, and rain in any quantity falls in October only. Thunder and lightning are very rare, notwithstanding the nearness to the mountains. In one word there reign all the winter, in the middle of the day, constantly clear blue skies, and there is hardly ever a day when the invalid cannot take a walk. It will look cloudy some mornings, but it will be sure to clear up by 10 a.m.

The sanitary condition of Nice is the best on the Riviera, and important measures are being perfected to make it equal, if not superior, to any city in the world. The water supply is excellent in quality and quantity.

Therapeutics.—Here we place in the front rank, on account of the dry, tonic, exciting air, all feeble subjects, whether from age or faulty constitution. Nice has been truly called "The providence of the aged and weak." All such subjects, and healthy old people, find that their temperature is easily kept up here, and a reaction is created by the stimulating air. We are convinced that many patients we have seen have prolonged their lives by residing here in winter. Dyspeptics do well; every one of them in the south gets a good appetite and assimilates his food well. The action of the light air and bright sunshine upon hypochondriacal and anæmic patients, is too well known to be more than mentioned. Diabetes, Bright's and skin diseases are all relieved, as the functions of the skin being better performed here than in the north, the work of the other organs is eased up. All women's complaints are vastly improved. The menstrual function is well performed in the south. Paralysis, rheumatism, sciatica and gout are constantly ameliorated. Scrofulous children, the respiratory affections, bronchitis, pharyngitis, laryngitis, &c., do well, and even

13

phthisis, under certain conditions, and in chosen situations. Liver and spleen complaints improve here where proper exercise can be taken. In regard to insomnia, while we admit that residence anywhere on the direct Mediterranean Sea shore is exciting, still we are convinced that no syrup of poppies can compare in sleep-producing power with sunshine and light, combined with exercises in the open air. Sunshine itself is the best soporific, it has the most potent influence; giving strength, beauty and cheerfulness. The climate, in short, is mild, and life is so rich in this sunny land, where the tonic sea air is redolent of flowers and maritime pine tree odour, that nearly all chronic maladies are benefited by it.

Contra-indications. — The only exception are certain forms of the mental or brain troubles, which should be submitted to proper examination by a competent specialist before being sent to the Riviera.

In this place we may refer again to the so - styled differential value of the winter resorts on the Riviera. It is not possible that in these few miles of coast any substantial difference of climate can exist. The fact is, that the warmer places, such as Beaulieu, Eza, &c., are very limited in extent, and are close under the hills. This is true also for a certain portion of Mentone and this accidental protection, or that afforded by a clump of trees, keeps off the winds from certain quarters, although they are all open to the sea coast, and the one is just as much subject to winds as the other. The large towns being built on the open plains, are not, of course, so well protected by hills, but away from the centre and close to the hills around Nice, we can assure all seekers after the exact truth that there exist . just as well-protected places as anywhere else, and that everywhere along this coast the climate is the same.

Nice has several distinct climatic zones; the Marine, by the sea-side; the Valley, by Longchamps and Carabacel and the near protecting hills. Then the hills themselves, as Cimiez, &c., where the climate is more sedative than in town. The environs of

Nice are exceedingly beautiful. Passing along the "Shelf," or Cornice road by the sea and over the mountains, is a drive that is a marvel of beauty and interest. In another direction, to St. André, we have a road that equals any part of Switzerland. Villefranche is a small village in twenty minutes' drive, where the fleets of the world meet in the great land-locked harbour. A late writer says :— "One comes to Nice to amuse oneself, to Cannes to live, and to Mentone to die ;" but like many smart sayings, this is not exactly the truth.

It would not be doing the place justice to forget to mention the sea-bathing, which is excellent in spring, summer and fall, and can also be used by hardy bathers in winter when the water is warmer than the air, and of course much warmer than that of the Atlantic coast. There are no waves to speak of, and the beach is pebble in front of the Promenade des Anglais, but sandy at the Lazaret.

Physicians. — Drs. Ashmore - Noakes, Brandt, W. A. Sturge and Gilchrist (English) ; Thomas Linn, M.D. (American physician), Quai Masséna, 16.

Dentists.—N. W. Williams and E. Frisbie, D.D.S. (Americans), M. Shillcock (English).

English Chemists.—Messrs. Nicholls and Passeron, Quai Masséna, 4.

Hotels. — Grand Hôtel, Cosmopolitan, France, Grande Bretagne, Des Anglais, Angleterre, Méditerranée, Luxembourg, Westminster, Des Princes, Paradis, St. Petersburg, Kraft's Grand Hôtel Nice, Des Palmiers, &c., Grand Hôtel Cimiez at Cimiez, Grand Hôtel Mont Baron.

Pensions.—International, Genève, Tarelli, Anglaise, Mrs. Buzby.

Booksellers.—Galignani's, Visconti's, Delbecchi.

Local English Books.—Dr. Linn "On Precautions for the Climate." See Anglo-American Guide to Nice. The New English Subscription Library at Credit Lyonnais Bank, contains some 3,000 volumes of the best works of travel, and everything relating to the Riviera.*

---

* *Beaulieu* is fifteen minutes by R.R. on the road to Mentone, fare less than a franc. By road over the

MONTE CARLO AND MONACO.

These two places, although quite different, are close to each other in this smallest principality in Europe, which measures about eight square miles. These stations are reached from Nice by the P.L.M.R.R. in about thirty-five minutes; two francs.

Monte Carlo itself is the most important place; although it cannot boast of 500 population it has a million visitors per year. It is extremely small, has almost no shops or streets, only a most beautiful garden, and a

---

hill by Villefranche in three-quarters of an hour, half a franc. By neighbouring hills. This pretty little place, with its neighbours *Eza* and *Turbie-sur-Mer*, are the best protected spots on this coast. It is so warm here that the place is called " Little Africa." It is close under the mountains that tower above it, while it is exposed to the full influence of the sun. Lord Salisbury passes some time here in his new Villa Bastide. Dr. Buderi, of Paris, has a house just below, and the whole country about here is being taken up rapidly by English and others for villas.

Hotels.—Besides the Grand Hôtels Anglais, Beaulieu and Metropole, other large establishments are

few roads running up the sides of the hill on
which it stands. They are lined by fine
hotels and good villas. It is one of the
most beautiful spots on the Riviera, but
is morally very ugly. Were it not for
the gambling tables it would become one of
the most popular health resorts along this
coast, as it is fairly well protected and warm
under the hills. The mean winter temperature is 48' Fah. It has excellent sea-bathing.

---

projected. The place is as yet but a village, no shops
or amusements but walking and driving.

Physician.—-Dr. Jais Durel.

It need hardly be said that all cases for which the
Riviera is suitable, do well here.

Ajaccio, in the Island of Corsica, can be reached
well from Nice by Morelli line of Steamers, leaving
every Saturday at 5 p.m. It is claimed that there is
but slight variation of temperature here, and but little
dust.

The climate is certainly an excellent one, the wind
being less than in the Riviera ; but the steamer trip
and the small number of English here makes its development slow. The mean humidity being greater
than the resorts on the French and Italian sides,
cases of dry bronchitis and asthma do well.

Hotel.—Continental.

Physicians.—Dr. Malgreni and Dr. Trotter (E.).

Monaco itself, and indeed Monte Carlo, close to the lower part near the casino, is exposed somewhat to winds, and there are no level walks.

Physicians. — Drs. Fagge, Fitzgerald, Hutchinson, and Mitchell (all English).

Hotels.—(All dear.) Princes, Beau-Rivage, Grand Hôtel, Anglais, Metropole, Russie, Prince de Galles.

MENTONE (ALPES MARITIME).

It is close to the Italian frontier and reached by the same line as that to Nice, one hour farther on; three francs from Nice. From London, £8, in twenty-two hours.

Mentone is fifteen miles from Nice, 154 miles from Marseilles. It is a small town of about 12,000 population. The coast line of the Maritime Alps here rise as high as 4,000 feet, making a sort of semi-circle of hills that give an almost perfect protection to one part of the town. For this reason that part of Mentone certainly has a milder climate than the rest of the larger stations on the Riviera.

We have before explained that the only difference in climate in any of the places from Hyères to Mentone is caused by the hills coming so close to the shore that they leave only room for a road and some houses squeezed in between the base of the mountains and the sea-shore, the more favourable place for warmth is at all times under the protection of the hills.   This is to be found, as we said before, at all the stations in more or less degree.   When there is any considerable valley opening out and bringing cool currents of air down from the screen of mountains which should keep off the north winds, it naturally follows that all within its influence must submit to a more or less cold climate.   There is also something in the fact that Mentone has rather bare limestone mountains over its sheltered part, and owing to the absorption of the sun rays by these rocks, and the gradual giving up of this heat during the night, the temperature is made higher than elsewhere.   The East bay at Mentone is called " A sun trap," and its hot relaxing air is not at all suitable to many persons ; certainly not for those who are fairly well and need bracing.   The sanitation is not first class.

Therapeutics.—Phthisis or consumption is certainly better treated by climate in Mentone than the other stations.   A careful study of each case must be made by a local physician. Scrofula, chronic gouty and rheumatic affections in those who like warmth and a quiet indolent life, laryngeal diseases, bronchitis, &c., and skin diseases do well here.

Contra - indications. — Epilepsy, nervous maladies of certain kinds, violent hysteria.

The mean temperature is for the six winter months 46° and for the whole year 61°. The dryness being 68 per cent. eighty-one days' rain in the whole year, twenty-four inches in all.   The drainage has been improved of late.   The walks are not good, being very hilly.   The place is exceedingly dull, being almost given up to invalids.

Physicians. — Drs. Fitzhenry, Siordet, Marriott and Stanley-Rendall (all English).

Booksellers.—Bretrand and Queyrot.   See " English Guide to Mentone."

Hotels.—National, Orient, Louvre, Princes, Isles Brittaniques, Ambassadeurs, Westminster, Grand, Bellevue, &c.*

PAU (BASSES PYRÉNÉES).

475 miles from Paris. Orleans and S. of F.R.R., seventeen hours, ninety-four francs. From London, £7.

We must now jump to the other side of France, and leave the Riviera to speak of *Pau* (pronounced *Po*). It has been for a long time recommended as a winter station; and upon this complex question of climate

---

* *Cap Martin* or Cape St. Martin. Looking to the left of Monte Carlo this promontory is seen like a great whale rising from the sea. It is covered with a forest of pines and olives, the ground sloping down to the sea on every side, and seems destined to a great future. This tongue of sand has just had a fine hotel built upon it. The Empress Eugénie has bought land there for a villa, and a number of English visitors to this coast have done the same thing. The cape is two miles west of Mentone, and can be reached by tramway from there and easily from Monte Carlo.

Hotel.—Cap St. Martin.

we wish to be entirely impartial.   Many writers recommending a certain place to the detriment of another will speak of temperature as all important.   Those who wish a winter station that is really hot should go to Senegal, Madagascar, &c., but the real influence of climate depends on a complication of circumstances.   For those who seek sunshine and fine weather, Pau is scarcely a fitting winter resort, as it has a tolerably severe winter.   On the other hand it has none of the sudden transmissions from cold to heat like Nice, and it is not windy.   The climate is sedative and humid.   The altitude is 660 feet.   The mean temperature is 42° Fah. for the winter.   There are 119 wet days. The atmosphere is still, and during the season much more rain falls than on the Mediterranean.   Frost, snow and cold nights are also seen in winter.   The town is in a fine situation on a plateau looking out on the Pyrenean hills, fifteen miles distant, 125 miles south of Bordeaux.   The sanitation is fair, and the hotels are good.   30,000 inhabitants. A good English club, fox-hunting and other gatherings in the English style, makes the place popular with English people.

Therapeutics. — Dry bronchitis, irritable, nervous complaints, emphysema, and all diseased states associated with increased nervous and vascular action.

Contra-indications. — Nervous debility or weakness, rheumatism. Those who feel depressed in a damp, dull place should keep away.

Physicians.—Drs. Bagnell, Hunt, Clay (all English).

Hotels.—France, Gassion, Beau Sejour.

Bookseller.—Ariza, Rue de la Préfecture.

PARIS (SEINE).

The great French capital (le beau Paris of the French) is certainly the most beautiful city in the world. It is 288 miles from London (£3). Population about 2,500,000, of whom it is estimated there are 12,000 English, and some 5,000 American residents. The English are in large part of the working classes ; the Americans are mostly abroad for pleasure or for health. The mean winter temperature of Paris is about 38° Fah., the annual 51°. The climate is temperate, not very severely cold in winter, and the summers are never extremely hot. The great city, however, is not suitable for invalids in winter, the winds being raw and chilly with much damp cold weather. The summers are not bracing.

Physicians.—(See Medical Directory for addresses.) American : Drs. Austin, Boyland, Clarke, Dunn, Good, and Warren-Bey. Oculist, Dr. Bull.

English : Drs. Barnard, Chapman, Dupuy, Herbert, Jennings, Loughnan, Prendergast, MacGavin.

(See Medical Directory, which also gives the addresses of the American and English physicians in Paris in full. See "Hints," page 14, for fees.)

PARIS (FRENCH) SPECIALISTS.

Surgeons. — Professors Lannelongue, Le Fort, Verneuil ; Drs. Segond, Campenon, Peyrot, Reclus, Péan.

Bladder Diseases. — Professors Guyon; Drs. Tuffier, Ricard, Fort.

Physicians. — Professors Germain Sée, Potain, Dieulafoy, Bouchard, Hayem, Jaccond, Peter, H. Huchard; Drs. Rendu, Dujardin-Beaumetz, Hanot.

Nervous Diseases.—Professor Charcot; Dr. Gélles de la Tourette, Dr. De Jerine.

Women's Diseases. — Professor Tarnier; Drs. P. Budin, Auvard, Doleris, S. Pozzi, Lutaud.

Medico - Legal and Hygiene. — Professors Brouardel, Proust.

Eye Diseases.—Professors Panas, Galezowski, Bull, Landolt.

Ear Diseases.—Drs. Loewenberg, Cartaz.

Throat.—Dr. Gouguenheim-Fauvel.

Children. — Professor Graucher; Drs. Hutinel, Legroux.

Syphilis.—Professor Fournier; Dr. Mauriac.

Skin Diseases.—Drs. Besnier, Vidal, Hallopeau, Quauquand.

Electricity.—Drs. Apostoli, Good.

N.B.—The French doctors do not speak English. It would be best to get a resident

English or American physician to act as an interpreter when needed.

Dentists.—Americans: Drs. Evans, Barclay, Daboll, Bogue, Michaels, Marcelin, Shelly, Davenport, Woodward, Crane.

English : Drs. Moore, Neech.

English-American Chemists.—Roberts and Co. and Beral, both Rue de la Paix ; Rogers, Rue de Havre.

GERMANY.

THE climate of Germany proper is something like that of the Northern States of America, but the winter's cold is modified by the moist Atlantic breezes. At Hanover notably the annual mean is 60° to 52°, and the mean of January is 24° F. The valley of the Rhine, at Bonn and Wiesbaden, even may be spoken of as the mildest part, but no place in Germany can be recommended for a winter station for delicate patients who have anything the matter with the respiratory passages. The mineral water Spas are crowded in July and August, and the treatment is thorough, long and tedious. At most of the stations there is a small "cur" tax to pay, which gives admission to reading rooms and casinos, and secures good music in the place. The systems of drainage, as a general rule, are bad, but in certain places they have been much improved in late years. Germany and Austria are favoured with good table water springs, very fortunately, for the ordinary or river water is often unfit to drink. Many of these springs, used for drinking at home, such as the Apollinaris, Friedrichshall, &c., are not visited as stations.

SULPHUR WATERS.

Aix-la-Chapelle, or Aachen.

251 miles from Paris, N.R.R. direct in nine and a-half hours ; cost forty-five francs. From London, £5.

Aachen waters are hot sulphur springs, 116° to 166° F. They are near the Belgium frontier, four hours from Brussels. They are strongly sulphurous, containing sulphuretted hydrogen, carbonic acid gas, chloride of sodium, &c. Inunctions of hydrarg are used with the baths, and the waters are also taken internally.

Therapeutics.—The specialities are syphilis, chronic rheumatism, skin diseases, gout and paralysis.

Aachen and *Burtscheid* make together the largest town watering-place in Europe, forming a single large city of over 100,000 population. It is indeed one of the chief cities of the Rhenish province in the German Empire. The altitude is 734 feet. The number of visitors 20,000. The baths are open all the year. May to September is, however, the principal season, and the most favourable time for such baths and treatment. It is rather a warm place, and the sanitary state is much like all the towns in Germany. The water supply has been lately improved at great cost to the city. The average temperature is 54° F., the number of rainy days 110. There are fine drives in the Aachen Wald or forest, but the city is not very lively or interesting. The treatment, however, is thorough and excellent ; this is one of the " serious " places. From an historical point of view the city is interesting, being Charlemagne's old home, and the cathedral claims special notice as a valuable museum of architecture.

As to walks, Aix is not like so many of the mineral water stations, a pleasant country village ; but the tramways are cheap, and one can get out of town very quickly.

Physicians.—(There are sixty of them ;

most of these speak English.)   Drs. Brandis, Schuhmacher, Schuster, Mayer, Lersch.

Hotels.—Grande Monarque, Grand Hôtel, Bellevue, Empereur, Unions-Hôtel, Dubigké, Kaiserhof.

Bookseller.—Rudolph Barth.   See " Aix-la-Chapelle as a Health Resort," in English, written by several doctors of the place.*

---

* *Weilbach*, about fourteen miles from Frankfort, has a cold sulphur spring, and so have *Langenbrücken, Neundorf, Eilsen* and *Meinberg*, but they are not frequented by English or American people.

SALINE SPRINGS.

Baden-Baden (Grand Duchy of Baden).

Route.—E. of F. by Strasburg, 354 miles, fourteen hours, sixty-five francs. From London, £5 9s.

There are thirteen warm chloride of sodium springs at Baden at a temperature of from 110° to 154° Fah. They contain sixteen grains of common salt to the pint, and it is said a little arsenic. They have no smell, and but little gas. The taste is not agreeable. They are diaphoretic, diuretic, laxative, and tonic, and excite the secretions. They resemble those of Wiesbaden, and have been recommended in many diseases, but they are of the order of waters called " Indifferent," and not remarkably efficacious.

Therapeutics.—Rheumatism, gout, gastric catarrh, slight cases of scrofula and malaria. They are also claimed for bronchial and other catarrhs of the respiratory tract, but for these cases the climate is somewhat variable. There is a very. fine establishment, the " Friedrichbad," with all hydro-therapeutic requirements. It contains baths of all kinds—Russian, pine, electric and swimming. There is also a section for Swedish massage and gymnastic movement treatment. These baths are open all the year ; the prices are fixed by the government. There are milk, herb and grape cures.

Baden-Baden is twenty-five miles south of Karlsruhe, six miles from the Rhine, and thirty miles from Strasburg on the River Oosbach. Its altitude is 650 feet ; population 14,000, and it receives a large number of visitors. Even now, since gambling is no longer allowed, as many as 50,000 people visit the place in summer. Its situation is charming, and its environs are certainly beautiful, built as it is on the Schlossberg-Hill and sheltered by the lower ranges of the Black Forest. It is a pretty summer place, and it has been for many years a favourite resort of the aristocracy of Europe. The races at Iffezheim are a great attraction in September, and the climate is warm and variable during the season. It rains a good deal. The sanitary arrangements are better than in many German places. The theatre, conversation house, balls and concerts are first-rate, and the promenades are excellent, the "Schloss," whence on bright days the cathedral at Strasburg can be seen, Eberstein Castle, the Hermitage, Falls of Allerheiligen, Geroldsau, &c.

English Church.—Rev. T. A. White, Langestrasse 33.

Physicians.—Heiligenthal, Berton, Oeffenger, Baumgartner.

Hotels.—Victoria, De France, Russie, D'Angleterre, Europe, Minérva, Bellevue, Badischer Hof.

The bookseller at Friedrich's Baths has local guides in various languages.

Expenses.—Baden is rather dear for Germany, but there are plenty of small hotels, such as the Trois Rois and Müllers, and many houses have furnished rooms to let, so living need not be dear.

NAUHEIM (HESSE-DARMSTADT).

454 miles from Paris, viâ Metz and Frankfort, sixteen hours; eighty francs. From London, £6.

These important salt water springs and works vary from 83° to 100° Fah., and contain carbonic acid gas. The taste is bitter and salt, yet the gas makes it agreeable to drink. One of these springs throws a jet forty feet high. Their high temperature, richness in common salt and carbonic acid gas make these waters tonic and laxative, while they are exciting to the skin.

They produce 17,000 quintals of salt per year. The gas being abundant, baths of it are given.

Therapeutics. — Scrofula, tuberculosis, lymphatism in general, chlorosis and anæmia, sciatica, gout and rheumatism, eczema, psoriasis.

Contra-indications. — As they determine congestion to certain organism, feeble people should not use them except under the doctor's orders.

Bad-Nauheim is twenty miles from Frankfort, and only a short distance from Homburg, but it is a very quiet place compared to its neighbour. Population, 3,000; 8,000 visitors. Altitude, 500 feet. The promenades are good, to Johannisberg, Ruins of Teichaus, Friedberg. The climate is mild in summer, with a light, bracing air.

Physicians. — Drs. Bode, Friedländer, Müller, Schott.

Hotels.—Kursaal, Europe, Bellevue, Pension Victoria.

HOMBURG.

477 miles from Paris. N. of F.R.R. viâ Cologne and Frankfort, eighteen hours, eighty francs. It is only ten miles out from Frankfort on the Maine in forty minutes rail, on a branch road. From London, £4 11s.

Waters.—There are five cold springs of saline ferruginous acidulated water, with a slight inky taste. The water is clear, and gas is seen bubbling up. In the Stahlquelle, or steel spring, there is considerable rusty deposit. Taken in small quantities they constipate, while in large doses they are slightly laxative but tonic. In the Elizabeth-Brunnen there are common salt and some lithia. Pine baths are given here in the handsome Kaiser Willhelms-Bad, but drinking the water is the usual treatment.

Therapeutics. — Dyspepsia, catarrhal troubles of stomach and intestines, liver diseases, chlorosis and anæmia, gout, malaria.

Contra - indications. — Congestion and hæmorrhages.

Homburg, called "Vor der Höhe," because it is at the base of the Taunus Mountains, altitude, 650 feet, has a population of 9,000; number of visitors, 12,000. The climate is bracing and healthy, rather cool and rainy, but drier in summer. The natural situation is not picturesque, but art has done much for the town, which consists of one rather ugly street. It cannot be said that it smells sweet; but the sanitation has been improved of late years. The pretty park and the woods and walks about the castle are all in its favour, as well as a splendid Kursaal left there, a survival of the gambling days, with its magnificent ball and reading rooms.

The place is quite English, and is said to have more English visitors than German. There are an English and a Scotch Church, twenty-five courts of lawn tennis, a golf ground, &c. The Prince of Wales is a frequent visitor here.

Physicians.—Drs. Schetelig, Deetz, Weber, Hoeber; twenty doctors in all. Most of them speak English.

Hotels.—Russie, Royal, Victoria, Bellevue.

Books. —·" Homburg and its Mineral Waters," by Dr. Schetelig, M.R.C.P. London.

KISSINGEN (BAVARIA).

554 miles from Paris, N. of F.R.R., viâ Frankfort and Würzburg, eighteen hours; eighty francs. From London, £5 1s. 9d.

Waters.—-Six cold saline springs. The " Rakoczy " is the best known. The water is not very limpid; it turns a bluish colour, and has a styptic taste. These are purgative, diuretic and exciting waters. Over 400,000 bottles are sent abroad per year. The whey cure is used here, and carbonic acid gas baths are given.

Therapeutics. — Atony of the intestines, gastric catarrh, dyspepsia, stomach complaints, amenorrhœa, scrofula, gout, nervous affections, malaria.

After-cures.—The iron waters.

Kissingen in the Saale, a healthy valley. Altitude, 640 feet ; population, 5,000 ; visitors, 20,000, from May to September. The climate is mild, although the air is rather close in summer and a little damp ; this, however, must be said of most of the German places. A handsome Kursaal and fine Kurgarten are popular. Bismarck is a frequent visitor. The surrounding country is pretty, and there are interesting excursions to Altenberg, Staffels, Bodenlaube and Kreuzberg. Bocklet and Brückenau are two iron springs only five miles off that are used as after-cures. The life in Kissingen is very quiet, not to say dull. The water is drawn up from the wells here by men, a different arrangement from that which is usual at most places, where neatly dressed girls hand the water to visitors. The sanitation is fair.

Physicians.—Drs. Dietz, Stöhr.   The old-fashioned custom here is to have open-air consultations under the trees.

Hotels.—Royal Kurhaus, Russie, Victoria, Angleterre, Kaiserhof.

Books.—Dr. Granville's " Kissingen, its Sources and Resources."

KREUZNACH (RHEINISH PRUSSIA).

E. of F.R.R., viâ Forbach, fourteen hours, sixty-eight francs.   From London, £5 15s. It is eight miles from Mayence, one hour or ten miles from Bingen on the Rhine.

Waters.—They are bromo-iodurated waters and used as the saline springs in general.

Therapeutics.—Scrofulus affections, female diseases, gout and skin diseases, fibroid tumours.

Kreuznach, called Soolbad-Kreuznach, is on the Nahe ; it has a population of 1,600, and some seven thousand visitors.   The season is May to October.   The climate is fairly mild.   This is a dull village, with a good casino, or Kursaal, on a wooded island on the Nahe. There are nearly a hundred villas around it. The cure is a long one, six weeks being considered necessary. The baths are given in the hotels. There is a small place called Münster am Stein near by which has saline waters. Good fishing and boating and fine excursions in the neighbourhood, but the place is rather distant for invalids. Living is not expensive here.

Physicians. — Drs. Engelmann, Jung, Strahl, Wolff, Lier, Weber.

Hotels.—Oranienhof, Schmidt.

SODEN.

440 miles from Paris, eighteen hours, N.R.R., viâ Frankfort. It is only a half hour on branch line from the city, and nine miles from Homburg. Höchst is the branch station.

Waters.—These springs have lately been much spoken of in England. There are twenty-four of them, and they resemble those of Homburg, but are stronger, being laxative and tonic.

Therapeutics.—The specialities are chronic

throat diseases, scrofula and the usual troubles treated at salt-baths.

Soden-am-Taunus is a pretty place in a valley surrounded by mountains. It is renowned for its roses and rich verdure. The altitude is 451 feet; population, 1,400. Soden claims to be a climatic station as well as a salt spring. Its climate is, in fact, quite soft and equable, and German invalids spend much time here in the open air in hammocks suspended from the trees which surround all the houses. The life here is very quiet and soothing, but by no means bracing. It is suitable for those who need sedation and calm, and it is becoming popular with the English invalids.. The promenades to Drei Linden, Koenigstein, Kronthal and its waters, Homburg, &c., are interesting.

Physicians. — Drs. Thilenius, Haupt, Hughes, Stoltzing, Fresenius.

Hotels. — Kurhaus, Colossus, Frankfurter Hof, Europe.

WIESBADEN.

405 miles from Paris, E. of F.R.R., viâ Pagny; fifteen hours, eighty francs. From

London, £21 14s. 9d. The waters are warm alkaline salines, 155° to 160°. The spring called Kochbrunnen is the type. It has fifty grains of common salt to a pint of water. The waters taste somewhat like weak chicken broth—very weak soup we should say.

Therapeutics.—Gout, catarrh of stomach and intestines, rheumatism, scrofula, skin diseases, liver and spleen troubles.

Wiesbaden is a city of 55,000 inhabitants; there are 80,000 visitors; the altitude is 360 feet. The baths are given all the year round, but like all such places it is most frequented in summer.. This station does not rely only on its waters, but gives milk, whey, grape, compressed air and massage cures. It is also proud of its many excellent cheap amuse-ments, and of its educational resources. It even claims to be a winter station for climate, but this is hardly to be admitted. In summer the climate is very hot, mosquitoes being abundant, and it is cold in winter. It is said, however, that the cold is dry, being mostly accompanied by a clear atmosphere. The city lies in a broad open valley, protected on

15

the north and east by the Taunus hills, while it is exposed to the south. The streets are clean, wide, and well drained. The water is good, the sanitation very fair. The walks and drives are not so pretty as at Baden-Baden; but see Dietenmühle, Geisberg, the Mausoleum of the Duke of Nassau, Neroberg, &c. Drive also to Schlangenbad and Schwalbach.

English Church.—Frankfurter Strasse.

Physicians. — Drs. Pagenstecher, Ricker, Hezger, Pfeiffer, Hofmann and Ziemssen.

Hotels.—Quatre Saisons, Kaiserbad, Victoria, Grand, Hôtel Rose, Rhine. Many of the hotels are bathing houses, as the baths are to be had in private establishments as well as in the large central one.

ALKALINE AND INDIFFERENT WATERS.

Ems (Duchy of Nassau).

375 miles from Paris, viâ Cologne, N.R.R., sixteen hours; sixty-eight francs. From London, £3 19s.

Waters.—These are hot alkaline springs, 115° to 85° Fah. There are twenty of them.

Therapeutics.—The great treatment here is for catarrh of all kinds, bronchial and laryngeal; women's diseases, sterility, nervous dyspepsia, gout and many other troubles.

Bad Ems is on the Lahn, five miles from Nassau, altitude 300 feet; has a population of 8,000. The place is all hotels and lodging - houses. The number of visitors is 18,000. Milk and whey cures are used, as well as the terrain Kur. The climate is mild for central Germany, and the summers are hot and moderately moist. The baths have

been named "Violet," "Pearl," &c. The
natural situation is beautiful, with pretty
shaded walks. A covered way will be seen
here made for the late Emperor William.
The society is good, and the place quiet, with
excellent music. The railway up the Mühl-
berg, 900 feet, is useful, taking one up out
of the hot valley in summer. The health
reports are satisfactory. Many Russians come
here, as well as English and Americans.

Physicians. — Drs. Döring, Flottmann,
Geisse, Orth, Reuter and Vogler.

Hotels. — Kurhaus, Angleterre, Quatre
Saisons, Bristol, France.

NEUENAHR (RHENISH PRUSSIA).

N. of F., viâ Cologne, thirteen hours ;.
sixty francs. From London, £5 8s.

Waters.—These are excellent, warm, alkaline springs, 97° Fah.

Therapeutics. — Diabetes, chronic throat
and pulmonary affections, chronic Bright's
disease, gout, hysteria, &c.

Bad Neuenahr, altitude 760 feet, is in the

Ahr valley, between Bonn and Coblentz, on the left bank of the Rhine. The waters are weaker than those of Ems. It is a very quiet and cheap place, with a mild climate and no sudden changes, but there are some mists in the morning. The sanitary condition is satisfactory. Promenades to Altenahr, Landskron, 990 feet, Apollinaris spring and its mountain; fine Rhine scenery. There are fine new bath buildings here.

Physicians.—Drs. Schmitz, Teschemacher, Unschuld.

Hotels.—Kurhaus, Victoria, Hollande.

SCHLANGENBAD (HESSE NASSAU).

405 miles from Paris, E. of F.R.R., nineteen hours; seventy-eight francs. From London £6 2s.; five miles from station Eltville.

Waters.—Nine indifferent springs, 95° F. They have been called "liquid velvet waters;" they have a soothing effect on the skin, and are considered cosmetic. It is a ladies' bath.

Therapeutics.—Diseases of the nervous system, hysteria, neuralgia, skin diseases.

Schlangenbad is only eight miles from Wiesbaden, at an altitude of 950 feet. It is a very small place; population 500; but receives as many as 6,000 visitors some years. The name means serpent's bath, from a harmless snake caught here, the *Columber flavescens*. The climate is mild, but subject to variations. It is, in fact, a quiet secluded spot suitable to nervous patients. There are some picturesque shady alleys and walks in the forest, also to Rauenthal, Eberbach, Niederwald, &c.*

English Church service in Nassauer Hotel.

Physicians. — Drs. Baumann, Wolff, Grossmann.

Hotels. — Victoria, Berlin, Swiss, Royal, Casino.

---

* *Wildbad*, in the Black Forest, is another of these indifferent waters. It is used in baths only, and not frequented much by English or Americans.

IRON WATERS.

Pyrmont (Waldeck).

487 miles from Paris N.R.R., viâ Cologne, eighteen hours; seventy-eight francs. From London, £6 1s.

Waters.—These seven cold ferruginous springs are really compound chalybeate and saline waters, somewhat stronger than Schwalbach and St. Moritz. The taste of the Stahlbrunnen, or steel spring, is salt and bitter.

Therapeutics. — Anæmia and chlorosis, female complaints, atonic form of dyspepsia, hysteria. (Used like Kissingen waters also.)

Pyrmont is forty-five miles and two hours from Hanover on the Emmer; altitude, 400 feet; population, 2,000; visitors, 12,000. It is in one of the elevated valleys of North Germany. The climate is mild and healthy with, however, some sharp variations in the temperature. It is one of the oldest spas, but not the most picturesque. It is an agreeable and comfortable place, and not dear. The best excursions are, the Königsberg, Friedensthal, Hornberg, Exterstein, Dunsthöhle and its jet of carbonic acid gas.

Physicians. — Drs. Schücking, Köhler, Lynker, Seebohm.

Hotels.—Grosses Bad, Lippescher Hof, Krone, Waldecker Hof, Des Bains.

Books. — See Dr. Seebohm's "Pyrmont Spa."

SCHWALBACH, OR LANGEN SCHWALBACH (NASSAU).

408 miles from Paris, seventeen hours ; eighty francs. From London, £6 4s. Eltville Station, and then a drive of eight miles.

Waters.—They are cold iron springs and mud baths. They are charged with carbonic acid gas, and pleasant to drink.

Therapeutics.—Female complaints are the great speciality at this station. Anæmia and chlorosis, nervous diseases, sterility, exhaustion after confinement and loss of blood, hysteria, &c. After cure for Wiesbaden. It is the iron cure of Germany.

"*Before-Cure.*"—It is considered a good plan for patients to go first to Soden or Ems for a short cure before taking these waters. The trains in Germany are filled with travellers from one bathing station to another in summer. It is quite the habit with the Germans to take both "first cures" and "after cures."

Schwalbach, or Langen Schwalbach, so called owing to its long street of straggling houses, is 65 feet above the Rhine and 1,090 feet above sea; population, 3,000; and it has 7,000 visitors in the season, from May to October. Its situation is very pretty in a healthy valley surrounded by forests, having pleasant walks in them. The climate is rather pleasant after Wiesbaden's heat. The life is quiet, and little is to be seen but weak, anæmic ladies. There is, however, the usual Kursaal and its music and balls. Living is not dear. Promenades to Eisenhammer, Adolphseck, Hohenstein.

English Church.

Physicians.—Drs. Böhm, Grebert, Frickhöfer.

Hotels. — Metropole, Quellenhof, Duke Nassau, Berliner Hof.

SEA BATHING.

CUXHAVEN.

THIS bathing place is at the mouth of the Elbe, near Hamburg, in Hanover, on the North Sea. It is a pilot station for vessels arriving at Hamburg, and can be best reached by diligence from Bremerhaven and Geestemünde twice a day in six hours. It is a very pleasant little sea-side place. Dr. Hälssen.

Hotels.—Belvedere, Dolles.

HELIGOLAND.

This island is six hours by steamer from Hamburg, and five from Bremerhaven, but can be reached from Cuxhaven in two and a half hours. It is thirty-five miles from Cuxhaven in the North Sea, and only one mile wide, and has only lately been ceded to

Germany by England. It is a splendid sea-bathing place, having a good sandy beach. The cliffs are of red sandstone and are very picturesque, and when lit up show fine effects of light and shade. The population is 2,000; number of visitors, 10,000. It has excellent accommodation for bathers. The people are Friesländers, speaking an old dialect, which is an unwritten language, allied to the English. The island is, however, really German; it has the rare advantage of having sea air on all sides, making an insular sea climate suitable in certain cases.

Physician.—Dr. E. Lindemann.

Hotels.—London, Queen of England.

GERMAN AIR CURES.

GÖRBERSDORF.

N. of F.R.R., viâ Cologne and Berlin, to Dittenbach, and then a half hour's carriage drive; thirty-nine hours; 160 francs. From London £9 8s. Altitude, 1,700 feet.

Therapeutics.—Phthisis or consumption.

The great importance of air treatment in the scourge of consumption first effectively used in this country makes us place it in a separate chapter. The questions in regard to this treatment are by no means cleared up as yet. Dr. Brehmer asserts that Görbersdorf has never had any phthisis among its inhabitants, but it is not at all certain that a place where the disease does not originate is the best place to cure it. Cases have been cured, under certain conditions, on a sea voyage, or at the level of the sea. This place was the forerunner of the use of mountain resorts in winter, for the treatment of chest troubles. The air itself, douches, strict supervision of the diet, exercise and habits of the patients have here produced a greater percentage of cure than other methods. The climate is somewhat harsh and cold, but every attention to hygiene and good nourishment has worked wonders in these cases.

There is a similar establishment at *Falkenstein*, called Falkenstein im Taunus, near Homburg, in the Taunus range of mountains, altitude 1,800 feet; the place is well sheltered. Dr. Dettweiler, who conducts the cure, calls it *Curanstalt Falkenstein*. Cases of anæmia and convalescence are also received, as well as consumptives. To be " great in little things " is the motto in these establishments, and the success obtained is more a triumph of order, great care and hygiene, than of the locality itself. It is the careful, systematic regulation of everything relating to the invalid—food, exercise, repose, occupation, restraining morbid caprices, and the over sanguine tendency of persons suffering from phthisis that make the cures. *Life in the open air the whole twenty-four hours* is one of the great secrets. This system is spreading all over the world, and seems to be not only the best in consumption, but in many other complaints. See the Swiss resorts in the mountains, and the new sanatorium at Aix-les-Bains, on the Revard Mountain above that place, and elsewhere.

BERLIN.

The great capital city of the German Empire is twenty-three hours from Paris; 120 francs. From London £6 6s., viâ Dover, Brussels, &c. It has now 1,500,000 population, and would require a large book to describe it. Consult Guides to Europe.

MEDICAL SPECIALISTS (See Medical Directory).

Surgeons.—Prof. von Bergmann, Alexander Strasse 1. Dr. Hahn, Charlotten Strasse 59.

Physicians.— Prof. Leyden, Thiergarten Strasse 14. Dr. Oppert, M.R.C.P. Lond., Ring Strasse, Friedenau.

Eye Diseases. — Dr. Fröhlich, Oranien Strasse 47. Dr. Schweiger, Roon Strasse 6.

Ear Diseases.—Dr. Dennert, Alexander Strasse 44. Dr. Lucae, Voss Strasse 32.

Women's Diseases.—Dr. Gusserow, Roon Strasse 4.

Nervous Diseases. —Dr. Eulenberg, Lützow Strasse 60.

Children's Diseases.—Dr. Baginski, Potsdamer Strasse 5.

Throat and Chest Diseases. — Professors Fränkel, Neuesbad Strasse and Kirch Strasse 12. Dr. Fränzel, Karlsbad Strasse 3. Dr. Schötz, Potsdamer Strasse 20.

Hotels.—Royal, Continental, St. Petersburg, Rome, Europe, &c.

GREAT BRITAIN.

In England, Ireland and Scotland there are many health resorts that deserve more attention, if it were only for the language, than they usually get from English-speaking travellers in Europe; but there is a prevalent idea that one must go to the Continent. We are quite certain from a careful study that we have made of the springs and baths of Great Britain, that well-selected cases would be treated with advantage at these spas. They would, of course, have to be indicated by a physician knowing the patient well, as also the treatment in question. It must be admitted that the whole of this country is a very wet one, but this very fact makes one of its beauties. Nowhere else can be seen such dark-green, splendid freshness of vegetation. Then, while there is much humidity, there is a certain regularity of temperature, and never the extreme cold or raging heat of North America ; nor do the day and night temperatures present any marked difference. It may be called a damp, genial, mild climate. Most of the towns and cities have superior sanitary arrangements, better as a rule than those of the Continent ; so that Great Britain is a healthy residence for strong, well people. The death-rate is low. The mineral springs are not so well improved, in some instances, as those abroad, nor are they so important as a whole ; but there are some excellent places which we will mention. The summer sea-side stations are bracing in climate, and are numerous all round these islands. There are winter resorts which possess advantages for those who cannot go so far as the French Riviera ; and indeed they have indications in certain diseases that make them equal, if not superior, to some of the winter stations abroad.

SULPHUR SPRINGS.

HARROGATE (YORKSHIRE).

198 miles from London, on North-Eastern R.R., six hours, £1 9s. No less than 120 trains a day. It is twenty miles from York, and eighteen from Leeds.

Waters.—There are over eighty springs of sulphurous saline and also chalybeate waters. They are considered stimulant and aperient. The baths and all arrangements are first-class. The new bath hospital cost £30,000. These waters are like those of Uriage in France.

Therapeutics.—Chlorosis, anæmia, herpes, obesity, womb complaints, hepatic troubles, lead poisoning, gouty and rheumatic affections.

The place consists of High and Low Harrogate, and has a population of 5,000; altitude, 400 feet. It is built on an elevated plateau, and very few towns in England have such pleasant walks and drives. From Harlow Hill Tower the view extends for as much as sixty miles on a fine day. The excursions to Knareborough, Ripon, Studley, Fountain Abbey, Bolton Abbey, &c., are fine. The pretty "Stray" or common of 200 acres around the town is a feature here. The death-rate is 13 per 1,000 only. The sanitation is excellent. There is an irrigation farm of 322 acres, making it one of the best-sewered towns in England. The winter temperature is 39°. Harrogate, like many English places, is wanting in the light amusements, music, &c., of the French and German spas.*

Physicians.—Drs. Oliver, Ward, Hinsley Walker, and Johnson-Lavis.

Hotels.—The Queen's, Crown, Prince of Wales, Adelphi.

Books.—"The Harrogate Waters," Dr. George Oliver, and Dr. Johnson-Lavis, Harrogate, "Prescribers' Guide."

---

* There are other sulphur springs of smaller importance at *Gilsland, Shap, Dinsdale-on-Tees,* &c.

CHELTENHAM (GLOUCESTERSHIRE).

113 miles from London; Paddington Station, viâ Gloucester; four hours, 14s.

Waters.—These are sulphate of magnesia springs, and are used as an aperient.

Therapeutics. — Hepatic and portal inactivity, constipation, &c.

Cheltenham waters, like Hunyadi Janos, Pullna, Friederichshall, and other cold, aperient waters, are more drunk at home than at the springs. Still, quite a number of people frequent this resort. The city is a large and well-built one, population 40,000, with fine houses and clean streets. The climate is mild, having a considerable rainfall; it is considered relaxing. Living is reasonable in price. The sanitation is good, being worked by a *sewage* company, and a refuse-destructor is used.

Physicians.—Drs. Abercrombie, Bennett, Cottle, Roch.

Hotels.—Plough, Queen's, Royal, Lamb.

LLANDRINDOD (WALES).

There are sulphur, saline and iron wells at this place. The situation is on an elevated plateau ; altitude, 800 feet.

Physician.—Dr. Davies.

MOFFATT (SCOTLAND).

This sulphur station is in Dumfrieshire, in the south of Scotland, in an interesting country ; altitude, 400 feet. Fine invigorating air.

Physician.—-Dr. W. D'Oyly Grange.

STRATHPEFFER.

This station is at the foot of Ben-Wyvis in Ross-shire, near Dingwall. It has three sulphur springs. Mud baths are used here.

Physicians.—Drs. Manson-Middleton, and Fox.

See " Strathpeffer Spa " by Dr. Fortescue Fox.

LISDUNVARNA (IRELAND).

In County Clare, Ireland, is another of the sulphur waters of Great Britain. We simply mention these waters, as they are not at all frequented by travellers in Europe.

The well-known *Epsom springs* are in Surrey, but the place is little used as a watering-place.

————

SALINES.

THIS group of waters is the most interesting in Great Britain. They are all used in chronic rheumatism, gout and joint troubles, as well as scrofulous affections. We give a short account of the principal springs.

DROITWICH (WORCESTERSHIRE).

Three and a half hours from London ; open all the year. These are good saline waters, the brine being ten to twelve times as strong as ocean baths.

Therapeutics.—Rheumatism, gout, scrofula, syphilis.

Hotel.—Royal Brine Bath.

LEAMINGTON.

103 miles from London, three hours, 16s.

It is near Warwick, and has fine streets and parks, and four saline springs ; 28,000 population ; equable but humid climate. The waters are more purgative than the other salines in England.

Physicians.—Drs. Wilmot, Holmer, Thursfield.

Hotels.—Regents, Bedford, Crown.

MATLOCK (DERBYSHIRE).

144 miles from London ; four hours ; 19s. 2d. Midland R.R. ; St. Pancras Station.

This is called the Switzerland of England. It is situated on the wooded side of Derwent valley ; average rainfall, forty-one inches ; death-rate, thirteen per 1,000. It is largely visited by excursionists, over 250,000 per year ; but the bathers are not so numerous. It is a pleasant summer resort.

Physicians.—Drs. Wm. B. Hunter, Whitby.

Hotels.—Royal, Tyack's Bath Hotel, Devonshire.

WOODHALL SPA (LINCOLNSHIRE).

Three hours from London, one from Lincoln.

Claims to have bromo-iodine saline springs, and is perhaps the most important saline spring in England. Dull, flat country, but healthy.

Therapeutics.—Scrofulous joints, skin diseases.

Physician.—Dr. C. J. Williams.

Hotel.—Victoria.

———

ALKALINE AND INDIFFERENT SPRINGS.

BATH (SOMERSETSHIRE).

105 miles from London, Paddington Station, in only two and a quarter hours, 18s. ; nine trains a day.

Waters.—These are the only important hot springs in England (104° to 120° F.). They are called earthy or indifferent, and contain sulphate of lime. There are four large bath establishments. The doctors here have taken a leaf from Aix-les-Bains experience in late years, have imported *masseurs* and *masseuses* from that station, and have erected a new bath establishment to carry out the Aix or massage system.

Therapeutics.—Gout, rheumatism, palsy, old wounds, eczema (dry form), lumbago, sciatica.

Contra-indications.—Those of very hot waters in general ; plethora, hæmorrhages, &c.

Bath is a city with a population of 54,000, and 12,000 visitors per year ; situated on both sides of the Avon, twelve miles from Bristol ; altitude, thirty feet. It has a fine park and excellent squares of dark green gardens surrounded by good houses built of marble. The climate is moist but mild, 3° to 5° F. warmer than London. The English go mostly in the autumn and spring to Bath, as they consider it relaxing in summer. Living is very reasonable. The Abbey Church with Beau Nash's tomb, Victoria Park, and the ruins of old Roman baths are local sights. Beckford Tower, Hampton Park, Badminston and Bristol are good excursions.

The sanitation is good ; no cesspools are allowed in the city. The house drainage connects directly with the main sewers, and the large water supply ensures the complete flushing of drains and sewers, which latter are ventilated at different points. Death rate, nineteen per 1,000. There is great longevity in Bath. In 1889, 119 people died aged over eighty.

Physicians.—Drs. Brabazon, Spender, Budd.

Hotels.—Grand Pump Room, York, White Hart, Grand, White Lion, Lansdown Grove, Private Hotel.

BUXTON (DERBYSHIRE).

177 miles from London, Midland R.R., St. Pancras Station ; four hours, viâ Derby, £1 1s. 8d. ; second class, 18s. 3d.

Waters.—These springs are called " Simple Waters," 82° Fah. ; carbonate of lime being the principal constituent.   It is said that they contain nitrogen gas.

Therapeutics.—Stomach and bladder complaints.   Gout and rheumatism, neuralgia, sprains.

Buxton has 1,800 population; altitude, 1,000 feet; amid the finest scenery of the Derbyshire Wye, pure air and bracing, but rainy.   The drainage is good, and mortality very low.

The environs have most beautiful excursions to Chatsworth, Haddon Hall, Pooles-Hole, Diamond Hill, &c.

Physicians.—Drs. Bennett, Flint, Turner, Robertson.

Hotels.—St. Ann's Old Hall, Shakespeare, Wood Eagle.

Books.—See "Buxton, Its Baths and Climate," J. Heywood, Paternoster Row, London.

CLIFTON (GLOUCESTERSHIRE).

Great Western R.R., Paddington Station, 118 miles; two and half hours, viâ Bristol; 18s.

Waters. — Alkaline carbonate of lime springs, used mostly as a diuretic.

Therapeutics. — Kidney and bladder troubles, gravel, vesical catarrh.

Clifton is one mile from Bristol; population, 22,000. There are 161 days of rain per year. The climate is soft and mild, and the baths are used all the year. The environs are charming. Excursions to Brandon Hill, Zoological Garden, &c. Season, May to September.

Physician.—Dr. E. Williams.

Hotels. — Bath, Royal, Queen's, Clifton Down.

IRON SPRINGS.

TUNBRIDGE WELLS (KENT).

THIRTY-TWO miles from London, viâ Folkestone, one hour, 7s. 6d.

Waters. — They are cold, bicarbonated, ferruginous springs.

Therapeutics. — Anæmia and chlorosis, leucorrhœa, women's complaints.

Tunbridge has 27,000 population, and is a clean, agreeable town, with pretty houses built on the hills, and surrounded by gardens. It has the reputation of being very dull and respectable. The soil is absorbent sandstone, and the climate is colder and more bracing than London, while it is not so rainy as the capital. Excursions to Penhurst, Bridge Castle, Bayham Abbey, &c. The death-rate only thirteen per 1,000. It is more noted for fine air than for its waters.

Physicians.—-Drs. Rix, Rankin.

Hotels.—Royal Sussex, Royal Kentish, Calverley, Mount Ephraim, Castle.

SEASIDE RESORTS.

NATURALLY the tight little islands of Great Britain have a very large number of these places all around the different coasts. *Queenstown, Aberystwith, Scarborough, Cowes, Dover* and *Folkestone*, then *Brighton, Ramsgate* and *Margate* are the best known. There is a much greater variety than in France. If a bracing place is wanted, the east and south-east coasts ; if a milder and damp place, then the west. The beach is also better as a rule than in France, as the sands are smoother. The expense is certainly less, but when we come to amusements it must be admitted that the English seaside places, if we except Brighton, are dull when compared with those of France. Most of the seaside places are also winter climatic stations, and will be found under that head. To all these stations the distance per railway is only a question of a few hours, and as they are not much frequented by the traveller in Europe, we do not give a separate description of each place.

WINTER CLIMATIC RESORTS.

THE value of the English winter resorts is difficult to explain in a few words. Tempera-ture alone is often deceptive. Dryness of the air is what should be sought, for it is generally acknowledged that humidity of atmosphere is highly detrimental to patients suffering from diseases of the lungs and chest. Unfortunately, Great Britain cannot boast of dry air, but all the same it has some excellent warm climatic stations, such as *Bournemouth, Eastbourne, Hastings, St. Leonards, Ilfracombe, Penzance, Torquay, Ventnor*. These, as we have said, are mostly seaside places, which makes them more equable than inland places. They are supposed to afford almost complete immunity from colds, but this depends somewhat on local conditions. The map of the world shows us that the territory of Great Britain is very small, and if we study the weather statistics, we find that the temperature will not vary more than one to two degrees all over the country, from the so-called warm winter resort to the north or cold places. We give a few of the official figures from the *London Meteorological Society's* statistics :—

	Winter.	Summer.
Torquay	43°, 5′	55°, 9′
London	42°, 4′	58°, 1′
Eastbourne	42°, 2′	56°, 2′
Ventnor	44°, 2′	57°, 2′
Bath	40°, 2′	53°, 5′

There is such a thing as the "personal equation" in temperatures; that is to say, whether the patient actually feels cold or hot in certain places. The rainfall is also an important factor. It is in London 182 days per year; Torquay, 177 days per year; Eastbourne, 165 days per year; Bath, 191 days per year; Falmouth, 204 days per year; Scarborough, 195 days per year; Bournemouth, 164 days per year. This last is the lowest figure given, and means that at the best it rains almost three-quarters of the year in Great Britain. Much is claimed for the very good systems of drainage in force in many English towns, and the relatively low death rate, the average at Hastings being only 17 per 1,000, at Eastbourne 18. The temperature is also remarkably equable, and soil often porous and sandy, allowing the great rainfall to be carried off rapidly. The water supply is most excellent.

Ventnor, on the southern shore of the Isle of Wight, has become a popular health resort in winter for pulmonary patients. It

17

has a National Hospital for Consumptives; it is on the famous Undercliff.

Bournemouth, £1 1s. from London; 110 miles; three hours; is also well known as a winter station. Winter mean temperature 41°. It has good villas built in the midst of pine trees. The sea-bathing is good. Beautiful pleasure gardens in the valley along the course of the *Bourne*. Sanitation excellent.

Torquay, 220 miles from London, £2 2s., is said to be the driest of all these stations, but this must be understood to be comparative. "If, for instance, we compare it with Hyères," says Dr. Yeo, "we find that the rainy days are 177 per year, while the south of France resort has 63."

Falmouth is warmer than Pau. The *Scilly Isles* have a more equable temperature than Nice.

Having said this much, it is evident that none of these places possess a dry winter climate; but they have a humid, equable one that is fairly mild and suitable to certain cases. We do not conceal from our readers the fact that the best English writers themselves admit that a good winter residence depends on its number of fine dry days, as well as on its mildness of temperature, and the fact that Great Britain has an average of 200 rainy days in the year, while 70 is the utmost in the Riviera, makes the superiority of the south of France beyond question. Having fairly considered the question of English winter climates, we do not hesitate to advise actual chest invalids to cross the channel whenever possible.

LONDON.

The great capital is in no way a health resort. We may say, however, that the sanitation is good and the death-rate low, which, considering the climate and the fogs, is astonishing.

MEDICAL LIST.

(See Medical Directory for addresses and complete list.)

Surgeons.—Professor Holmes, Sir J. Paget

V. Horsley, T. Bryant, J. Savory, Messrs. Nunn, P. Gould, C. Heath, Sir J. Lister.

Physicians.—Drs. Broadbent, Sir R. Quain, J. S. Bristowe, Mitchell Bruce, Lauder Brunton, F. Roberts, Sir A. Clark, Sir Dyce Duckworth, McNeill, Whistler, Dr. Sansom.

Chest. — Dr. Theo. Williams, Douglas-Powell, J. C. Thorowgood.

Throat.—E. Woakes, Dr. M. Hovell, Dr. Semon.

Heart.—A. E. Sansom.

Nervous Diseases. — Drs. Hughlings-Jackson, Dr. Bastian, Dr. Gowers, S. Wilks.

Children's Diseases.—Dr. Cheadle, Thomas Barlow.

Eye Diseases.—Power, C. Higgins, M. M. McHardy, Mr. Critchet.

Ear Diseases. — Dr. Pritchard, W. L. Purves, Sir William Dalby.

Women's Diseases.—Sir S. Wells, Dr. Barnes, Braxton Hicks, Sir W. Playfair, Macnaughton Jones.

Skin Diseases. — Jonathan Hutchinson, Radcliffe Crocker, S. Mackenzie, R. Liveing, A. Sangster, G. Thin.

Medico-Legal and Mental Questions.—Dr. Ferrier.

Hygiene and Diet.—Dr. Pavy.

Bladder Diseases.—Sir H. Thompson, Sir William MacCormac.

Mineral Waters and Health Resorts.—Dr. Hermann Weber, Dr. Yeo.

ITALY.

No climate in the world has been so favourably misrepresented as the Italian. Poets and novel-writers have raved of the "blue skies of Italy" so much, and have still such a strong influence in the matter, that people cannot understand that it is not true. Writers have made health resorts of many a place that has not the slightest right to be such. Florence, Rome and Pisa are examples of these popular errors. North Italy is very cold in winter. Turin has as severe a winter as Berlin. Florence has extremely cold winds; the Apennine hills around the city are mostly covered with snow all winter, and the wind coming over them is icy.   It has, in fact, a bad winter climate. On the south side of Italy, however, we meet the maritime type of climate, mild in winter ; and when protected by the mountains from the north and east winds, the stations on the eastern Riviera are nearly, if not quite, equal to the western in certain features.   As low down as Naples snow and frost are rare, while at San Remo they are almost unknown. The month of June is usually the best time to visit Italy.   At that time invalids can go there, as the climate is calm and serene by that month.   Italy can boast of some excellent mineral water springs, but the summer temperature of the country prevents its baths ever attaining the popularity of those of France and Germany.   This is indeed the reason why the Italian summer stations are not frequented by English and Americans ; they are too warm for them.   Indeed, the Italians themselves are in the habit of going to the French baths, and even to Germany, when they take mineral water cures.   This seems rather curious when we remember that Italy was the home of the ancient Romans, who first made use of mineral waters, and builded *thermæ* all over Europe, as the interesting remains found in so many of the stations prove. But the fact remains that though there are some excellent springs from the Apennines clear down to the foot of Vesuvius, they are but little used in comparison to the fashionable baths in other parts of Europe. We therefore give but a brief sketch of some of the more important stations in Italy.

SULPHUR WATERS.

Acqui (Province of Alessandria).

578 miles from Paris, viâ Turin, P.L.M.R.R., twenty-three hours; 100 francs. From London, £7.

Waters. — These are hot (169° Fah.) sulphur waters, and they use the fango, or mud baths also.

Therapeutics. — Arthritis, rheumatism, paralysis, skin diseases.

Acqui is only twenty miles from Alessandria, in Piedmont; population, 12,000. It is the capital of Montferrat, on the left bank of the River Bormida; altitude, 450 feet. It is in a very pretty country, with a healthy but variable climate. It is hot in summer and somewhat humid from the vapours coming from the springs.

Physician.—Dr. Dom.

Hotels. — Grand Hôtel, New Grand, Thermes, Italia.

VALDIERI (PIEDMONT).

583 miles from Paris, viâ Turin, twenty-eight hours; 110 francs. From London, £7 8s.

Waters.—They are weak sulphur springs, 180° Fah.

Therapeutics.—Rheumatism, ulcers, scrofula.

Valdieri has a population of 2,500, and is 4,100 feet altitude above Nice; fifteen miles from Coni. It has a good establishment, is in a mountainous country, and is cool in summer. The hotels are very moderate in charges. The mud baths are used here. The season is June to September. It is an excellent resort for people who winter in the Riviera. It can be approached from Nice through the Vesubie Valley, by a diligence, in twenty-four hours. Grand scenery over the Col de Tende. The new R.R. is now built on the Italian side to *Limone*, so that this interesting, high climatic station will soon come into repute for the air, as well as for its waters. The Nice doctors know the place well, and some of them summer at it every year.

Hotel.—Grand Hôtel, Valdieri.

———

INDIFFERENT WATERS.

LUCCA (TUSCANY).

740 miles from Paris, viâ Turin and Pisa ; thirty-four hours, 140 francs. From London, £8 12s.

Waters.—These are indifferent springs, temperature, 116° Fah. ; ten wells and mud-baths. Said to be like the waters of Bath, England. They are somewhat diuretic. The *stufa* or steam-baths are given here.

Therapeutics. — Rheumatism, neuralgia, nervous diseases, liver diseases, malaria, uterine complaints.

Lucca itself is about fifteen miles from these baths of Lucca. The climate is cool in summer, temperate and constant. The place is much resorted to by Florentine society, and is not at all dear. June to September is the season. It is healthy, and the neighbourhood is picturesque, being in a beautiful valley.

English Church.

Physicians. — Dr. Gason (English), Dr. Georgi.

Hotels.—New York, Europe, America.

SALINE SPRINGS.

LA PORRETTA (PROVINCE OF BOLOGNA).

814 miles from Paris, viâ Turin, in thirty hours ; 160 francs. It is on the R.R. between Bologna and Pistoja.

Waters.—These are salt waters, something like those of Uriage in France; temperature, 85° to 100° Fah. They are slightly laxative. The baths here are a special feature, being built of the handsome white marble of the country. There is so much carburetted hydrogen in the wells that it has been used at times for the purpose of lighting the town.

Therapeutics. — Skin diseases, scrofula, rheumatism, liver and spleen diseases.

La Porretta is in central Italy, in the valley of the Reno, at the foot of the Apennine range of mountains; population, 3,500. The climate is variable, but fair and warm in summer. About 1,000 visitors come every summer.

Physician.—Dr. Castelli.

Hotels.—Locanda Nuova, Italia, Palazzino.

Ischia (near Naples).

655 miles from Paris, viâ Turin, Rome and Naples; forty hours, 215 francs.

Waters. — Those in use, called Porto d'Ischia, are close to the town. Sand-baths are given on the sea-shore.

Therapeutics. — Rheumatism and gouty affections, paralysis, scrofula.

Ischia is a small island in the Bay of Naples, twenty miles off ; one and half hours steamer ; population, 25,000 in all, but the town itself 6,500.   Its most important waters are at *Casamicciola*, about four miles to the west side of the island.   Exposed to the northerly winds in winter, it is a cool summer resort. The central mountain, Mount Ipomeo, is 2,600 feet in altitude.

Hotels.—Bellevue, Pisani's, Baths Hotels.

MONTE CATENI (PROVINCE OF LUCCA).

741 miles from Paris, viâ Turin and Pisa ; only eighteen miles from Lucca ; thirty-three hours ; 140 francs.

Waters.—These are the most important saline springs in Italy. They contain 185 parts of common salt, temperature, 90° Fah. They are laxative and tonic.

Therapeutics.—The diseases treated are, dysentery, ague, enlargement of liver and spleen, rheumatism, scrofula. It is called the Italian Carlsbad.

Monte Cateni has a population of 6,500, and is between Lucca and Pistoja, in the valley of the Nievole, one of the prettiest places in Tuscany. The air is pure and healthy, with magnificent views on every side; altitude, 900 feet. It has a warm, constant climate. Excursions to *Florence* and *Leghorn*, only two hours' distance.

Physician.—D. P. Casciani.

Hotels.—De la Paix, Villa Toretta.

ITALIAN SEASIDE AND WINTER RESORTS.

These places can be grouped together as they are at once seaside and winter resorts. The whole Mediterranean coast has a large number of these resorts, from the French frontier at Ventimiglia to San Remo, Bordighera, Alassio, Nervi, Spezia, Leghorn, and on down to Naples, where we find the islands of Ischia and Capri. The Adriatic side is not frequented.

Here we have to say that the Italian resorts are not sufficiently improved. We may at once admit that some of them are equal to those on the French side of the Riviera as regards sea-air and climate. But they one and all lack in attractions such as the French are clever enough to provide for visitors. This may be owing to the Italian character, and the other defects may be owing to want of sanitary science; while the language is perhaps also a reason. In any case, none of these places are resorted to as much as those on the French coast; and just as soon as Alassio is past the climate is no longer suitable for winter residence. Genoa is not possible as a winter resort.

San Remo (Riviera de Ponente).

San Remo is reached from Paris, P.L.M.R.R., in twenty-four hours; 130 francs. It is thirty-two miles from Nice, and eighty-five from Genoa on the other side. From London, £7 18s.

Therapeutics.—The climatic treatment of chronic pulmonary complaints. Incipient phthisis, throat and larynx troubles, rheumatism, Bright's disease, general debility.

San Remo is the most important place on

the Italian Riviera ; population, 18,000 ; visitors, 8,000. The death-rate is twenty-four per 1,000. The town is all up and down, being on a hillside. The air is bracing, it claims not to be so stimulating as other places on the Mediterranean coast, and therefore better suited for nervous people. The average winter temperature is 53° to 59° Fah., forty-eight rainy days in the year. Like all this coast, two-thirds of the year it is sunny. The *mistral* and *sirocco*, both are felt when they blow. The amphitheatre of mountains behind the town protects it better than most of the places on this side of the Riviera. The old town itself with its *loggias* and terraces is one of the quaintest in Italy. There are no level walks, all the streets are up and down hill. In summer the Italians use it as a seaside resort. It has a clay soil, and remains damp longer than Mentone. There is nowadays a large German element in all the Italian cities and places of resort. A sad memory attaches itself to San Remo, for it was here that the Crown Prince, afterwards the Emperor Friedrich III. of Germany for so short a time, died. There are very few drives, and mountain excursions are impracticable. The situation is not attractive. There are English and Scotch churches.

Physicians.—Drs. Freeman, Hassall, Kay-Shuttleworth (English).

Hotels. — Londres, Victoria, West-end, Bellevue, Royal.

Books.—Dr. Hassall's " San Remo Medically Considered."

BORDIGHERA.

This is the second place of importance on the Italian side of the Riviera, but the first from the frontier, as it is only three miles from Ventimiglia ; twenty-five miles from Nice, and ten from Mentone. It is on the old Cornice Road, and is a very quiet little town amid palm-trees, with ready access to plenty of shade, which is unusual on the Riviera. The groves of olive and orange-trees here are remarkable. Population, 3,500. Dr. Goodchild says that its position on a promontory makes it get the sun 'sooner and retain it longer than the other places on the coast, but it also makes it windy. It suits cases who need rather bracing sea-air, scrofulous children and convalescents ; but it is much too exciting for nervous cases. The fact that Bordighera is on a neck of land gives it its distinguishing quality—"its sea-breezes make it tonic and bracing." The walks under the many trees of the place are delightful. Its temperature is much the same as the rest of the coast.

Physicians.—Dr. Goodchild (English), Dr. Herschel.

Hotels.—Belvedere, Angleterre, Londres, Beau Rivage.

Books.—Hamilton's " Bordighera and the Western Riviera."

Ospedaletti and *Alassio* are the only other two places that deserve mention on this coast. Even they are not yet developed, and except that the first is known as being two degrees warmer than the other stations, they are so small that they do not call for special mention. In time, no doubt, they will prove to be excellent winter resorts.

18

Hotels at Ospedaletti.—Reine, Pension Suisse.

Hotels at Alassio. — Grand, Rome, Londres.

Physician.—Dr. Dickinson (English).

PEGLI.

Pegli, six miles from Genoa, is sometimes praised as a winter station for asthma, but really has no claim to be such in comparison to the other resorts mentioned.

Hotel.—Grand de Pegli (see Villa Pallavicini).

GENOA.

Genoa itself, "La Superba" of the Italians, is certainly a fine city, and the newer parts should be spoken well of, but it is agreed by all writers that it is not a suitable place for invalids who have any pulmonary affection. It is a most interesting city for travellers in good health, but we are not writing for them, and must refer them to local guides. Climate variable ; cold winds and rains.

Physician. — Dr. Breiting (has English diploma).

Hotels.—Grand, Londres, Metropole.

NERVI.

Leaving Genoa by the Pisa-Florence R.R. we come in twenty minutes to this pretty little place just six miles out of town. We are now on the Eastern Riviera, or Riviera de Lavante.

Nervi has not nearly so high a winter temperature as Mentone, but there is less wind and more humidity, making it suitable to certain cases. The vegetation is almost tropical, and beautiful gardens are seen. It is a very quiet place for invalids who need repose. There are not many walks or excursions to be made, owing to the steepness of the roads beyond the little town. Population, 5,000 ; fifty-four rainy days, December to April. Many German visitors come to the place.

Physician. — Dr. Schetelig (M.R.C.S. London).

Hotels. — Anglaise, Oriental. Prices reasonable.

SPEZZIA.

This is a famous port and arsenal with a population of 20,000. It is scarcely known outside of Italy, yet it has a mild climate, calm, fairly equable, and free from dust, but not protected from winds. Good sailing and boating. Very few English visitors.

Hotels.—Grand Croce di Malta, Rome.

PISA.

This city was once celebrated as a wintering place, but did not deserve its repute, and has completely lost its vogue. It well deserves its name of "*Pisa Morta*," being now, save for its architecture, completely devoid of attractions; it does not deserve notice by invalids. The climate is damp and rainy, dark and cold, while the hygiene is very bad indeed. See the Leaning Tower, the Cathedral and the Campo Santo, and leave the place as soon as possible.

Hotels.—Grand, Angleterre.

VIA REGGIO.

On this coast may be mentioned the above little seaside place. It has a fine sandy beach, and is much resorted to in summer by the Florentines; and were it not for its mists would be a good winter station of the second class. Mild climate; fine pine-woods. *Hotels.*—New York, Anglo-Américain.

FLORENCE.

This large city comes next in our way through Italy. It is hard for us, who know the place well, to understand why invalids were ever recommended either to Pisa or Florence. Robley Dunglison, as far back as 1857 said: "This agreeable city is by no means a favourable residence for any class of invalids. It is subject to sudden vicissitudes of temperature, and to cold, piercing winds coming over the snow-clad Apennine Mountains, which suddenly change a warm summer day to a penetrating cold one." The bright, clear sun that is felt on some days has caused poets to rave about this city, and they have created a false impression of its climate that years of scientific observation have not entirely dissipated. It is said that, some cases of asthma do well in Florence, and robust persons might pass a short time there ; but we advise invalids to keep clear of it during the winter. It may be visited in June and September. There are English churches, and an American church.

Physicians. — Dr. Baldwin (American), Drs. Coldstream, St. Clair-Thompson and Wilson (English).

Dentists. — Elliott, Powers, Schaffner (Americans).

Hotels. — Italie, Anglo-American, New York, Royal, Grand-Bretagne.

ROME.

We feel that we must mention both Rome and Naples, although it is by no means certain that they deserve a place in a manual intended for invalids. It is certain, however, in regard to the medical aspects of Rome that far too much has been made of the Roman fever scare, and the tendency to pulmonary attacks in Italy. If the patients would not expose themselves to the risks of sight-see-.ing and fatiguing walks in cold, damp churches and picture-galleries, they would suffer little from the climate of Italy itself, as it is no worse than that of many northern cities. The best months for invalids to go to Italy are after May; June and September are excellent.

Physicians. — Drs. Gason, Thompson, Charles, Young, Spurway (English).

Dentists.—A. Chamberlain (American).

Hotels. — Quirinal, Bristol, Continental, Grand de Rome, Bellevue.

NAPLES.

The water supply now in the great southern city has been much improved, and the chances of zymotic poisoning are diminished, but the place is not one suitable to most invalids. The best months are June and September.

Physicians. — Drs. Gairdner, Barrenger, Johnson-Lavis.

Hotels. — Royal, Bristol, Grand, West-End, Rome, Victoria.

SPAIN AND PORTUGAL.

Madrid is spoken of as having weather that consists of " nine months of Hades, and three hot months in the year." Yet Spain, as a whole, has a fairly mild and healthy climate, with a considerable variety of conditions in the north and south. This is determined more by elevation than by geographical position. The chief mineral springs are in the Basque provinces, as also are the sea-bathing and climatic stations. Many of the mineral springs are very remarkable. The *Rubinat*, *Villacabras*, and *Carabana* waters give a splendid purgative effect from a very small dose ; and these waters, bottled, are destined to supersede the use of such waters as the Hunyadi Janos, &c. Then again, the re-markable springs containing nitrogen gas, not found elsewhere in Europe, should attract more attention than they do. With all this rich provision of excellent mineral waters and seaside resorts, Spain is not at all frequented by foreigners, and indeed, the rich Spaniard himself does not hesitate to cross the

Pyrenees for a spring-cure. This is largely owing to the fact that the spas are badly organized, and little comfort or amusement can be obtained at them. The Spaniard, in fact, does not know how to keep a modern hotel. The geographical situation may also have its influence. If Aix-les-Bains and Vichy were in Spain, it is not so sure that they would have such a large number of visitors.

As to *Portugal*, it has a fairly equable climate, being in fact a warm country; but it has a very heavy rainfall, over 200 inches a year. Fogs are also common in certain parts. It has some excellent sulphur springs; *Vidago* is considered by some as equal to Vichy as a mineral water station. Their remoteness, and the other reasons that prevent Spanish places from being frequented by Anglo-Americans, as much as they deserve to be, prevent these stations from being much used according to their intrinsic merits.

An exception must be made for Madeira, which is still made use of by the English as a climatic station.

We give a short notice of the most prominent places.

SULPHUR SPRINGS.

LEDESMA (PROVINCE OF SALAMANCA.)

855 miles from Paris, viâ Orléans R.R. and Salamanca, then coach for three hours : fifty-five hours in all ; 150 francs.

Waters.—They are hot, 86° to 122° F. sulphurous and very soft.

Therapeutics.—As of all such waters : rheumatism, paralysis, scrofula.

Ledesma springs are five miles from the town, on the left bank of the River Tormes, at the foot of an arid rock.   Life is very cheap and easy here, while the bathing arrangements are on a primitive plan.   Large swimming baths, or Piscines, are mostly used. Some 3,500 visitors come during the summer. The population is 1,600 ; altitude 2,500 feet. The climate is warm in summer, and suitable for such cases as frequent the baths.   Ledesma itself is a curious old Spanish town, surrounded by a Roman wall.   There are good excursions to be made in the neighbouring mountains.

Physicians.—Drs. Garcia, Lopez.

(ARCHENA, PROVINCE OF MURCIA).

1,160 miles from Paris, viâ Orléans R.R., to Madrid and Cartagena, fifty-one hours; 280 francs.

Waters.—They are clear and hot; they have a hepatic smell and taste and are exciting. These springs are considered a specific for syphilis by Spaniards, but their direct curative effect is not proved. It is probable that they have the usual action of sulphur waters in such cases. The temperature is 124° F.

Therapeutics.—Syphilis, scrofula, paralysis, skin diseases.

Archena is the best-known spring in Spain. The town is situated on the right bank of the Rio Segura: it has a good bathing establishment, with fifty mud-baths. Some 7,000 visitors in the season; altitude, 500 feet. Excellent climate all the year round. The excursions to Alameda and to Ricote are celebrated for the fruit trees. Blanca is a pretty village near by, with a fine mountain over it called Pina Negra, and a romantic Moorish castle at the top.

Hotel.—Fonda del Ré.

Physicians.—Drs. Zavala, Velasco.

CARRATRACA (PROVINCE OF MALAGA).

1,290 miles from Paris; viâ Bordeaux and Madrid; sixty-two hours; 326 francs.

Waters.—These important sulphur waters are said to contain also arsenic and iron. They are sedative to the nervous system and diuretic. They are not agreeable to drink.

Therapeutics.—Pulmonary and skin diseases are treated here; lupus, pellegra and acne.

Carratraca is also called *Ardales*. It is an Andalusian station, near Campellos, with a beautiful situation in a valley formed by the mountains of Bañs and Caparrain; population, 900; 3,000 visitors. It has a delicious climate. Season, June to September. The place is much visited from Malaga. It affords a good deal of amusement, and there are pleasant promenades.

Physician.—Dr. Salgado Y. Guillerno.

Hotel.—Fonda del Principe, Coleno.

IRON WATERS.

Santa Agueda (Province of Guipuzcoa).

575 miles from Paris, Orléans railroad to Zumarraga; then coach three hours; 110 francs; twenty-seven hours.

Waters.—Bicarbonate of iron (cold).

Therapeutics.—Anæmia and chlorosis.

The village is called Guesalibar, and the springs are in a very pretty valley, watered by the river Aramayouna, and dominated by a mountain called Murugain, 2,000 feet high.

———

ALKALINE AND INDIFFERENT SPRINGS.

Panticosa (Province of Huesca).

850 miles from Paris, viâ Irun to Huesca; twenty-four hours, 215 francs. It is twenty-four hours by coach and on foot. One can also get to Panticosa from Cauterets in France, by crossing a steep road, 8,000 feet high. Only one-half of the road can be gone over ·in a carriage; the rest must be

done on foot. People also drive to this curious place from Eaux Chaudes, in the French Pyrenees.

Waters.—These hot springs are oddly called after the disease the spring is supposed to cure; thus there is a liver spring, stomach, kidney, &c.

Therapeutics.—The maladies treated are numerous : catarrhs of the respiratory organs, cystitis, phthisis.

Panticosa is one of the highest and most romantic stations in Europe. It is 5,000 feet above sea level, in a narrow gorge surrounded by most magnificent mountains, and splendid chestnut and walnut trees. The road to it is called the *Escalar* or Stairway. There are over 2,000 visitors, notwithstanding the difficulty of getting up to the place. The village seems full of water, as there are waterfalls and little lakes on every hand. The climate is agreeable in July and August.

SALINE SPRINGS.

Cestona (Province of Guipuzcoa).

570 miles from Paris, viâ Madrid and Zamarrago, then omnibus in half an hour.

Waters.—They are chloride of sodium springs, salt and bitter to the taste, and slightly laxative.

Therapeutics.—Rheumatism. Catarrhs of all kinds are treated.

Cestona is also called Guesalaga or Salt-Water Place. It lies between two lines of mountains in an agreeable climate. As in most of the Spanish places, the hotels are called Fonda del Ré (King's Hotel), &c. There are excellent excursions and boating on the River Urola.

PORTUGUESE SULPHUR SPRINGS.

Las Caldas da Rainha (Province of Estremadura).

This is one of the most frequented stations in Portugal. It is on the railroad between

Lisbon and Leiria. The waters are sul-
phurous-salines, 92 F.

LAS CALDAS DE VIZELLA.

This place may also be mentioned as a
sulphur station. It is five miles from Gue-
maroës, on rail from Oporto to Vizella;
temperature 90° to 130° F. The scenery is
grand here. These hot waters are used in
rheumatism and skin diseases.

———

SALINE SPRINGS.

Rio Magor, near Santarem, are cold saline
springs, and *Monsao*, in the province of
Minho, are hot waters of this class.

———

IRON WATERS.

Of these springs, *Mirandela* (Tra los
Montes) and *Torres Vedros*, near Lisbon,
may be mentioned.

———

ALKALINE SPRINGS.

Vidago (Tras os Montes).

This is the Vichy water of Portugal; a pleasant place, mostly frequented in the autumn, September to November. The situation is picturesque, climate agreeable; trout-fishing.

Junqueiro.

This is the most important of the sea-bathing places in Portugal. It is on the Atlantic near Lisbon.

SEASIDE STATIONS.

San Sebastian (Bay of Biscay).

This is a most fashionable seaside place for the Spaniards. A number of foreigners come over from France to see the bull-fights. It is only twelve miles from *Irun*, the frontier. The beach is a fine sandy one, while the scenery is good, it being under Monte Orgullo. There are amusements of all kinds, and a fine casino.

19

Physician.—Dr. W. J. Smith.

Hotels. — Londres, Continental, Marten, Inglis.

ZARANS.

This charming little place is on the Cantabrian coast, fifteen miles from San Sebastian, and has over 7,000 aristocratic visitors during the bathing season. It was the Ex-Queen Isabella's favourite resort in summer.

Grand Hotel.

———

WINTER CLIMATES.

MALAGA.

This is about the only place in Spain that has serious claims to attention as a winter climate. It is thirty-six hours only from Paris, and twelve from Madrid. The city is built on a flat sandy plain, and its streets are pent-up and narrow, and prevent the sun from reaching the houses. The sanitary condition is not satisfactory. This much said, however, it must be admitted that the climate is a dry, equable one. The mean winter temperature is 56° Fah. The winds are sometimes trying; rainy days in winter, forty; population, 135,000.

Physician.—Dr. Bundsen.

Hotels.—Victoria, Europa, Alameda.

MADEIRA.

These five well-known islands are 1,332 miles from Southampton, and 535 miles from Lisbon. Steamers arrive there from the English ports of Southampton and Liverpool in five days; Hamburg, Germany; Havre, France, and Lisbon. The last is two days off, the voyage costing 200 francs; from the other ports about double (375 francs).

Therapeutics. — Early phthisis, chronic catarrhal complaints, scrofula. Diarrhœa is contra-indicated, as there seems to be a liability to this trouble in the country.

These Portuguese islands are mountainous masses of volcanic formation, and much up-and-down hill. The climate is warm, humid, and equable, and a pleasant winter one.

Mean winter temperature, 60° Fah. Rainy days, eighty - eight. Population, 131,000. Seventeen degrees warmer than London, five warmer than Mentone. Great uniformity of climate. There are few cloudless days.

Funchal is the capital, population, 20,000. It has a soft, soothing climate which has been rather under-rated, but is now coming into favour again for certain cases of irritative bronchial troubles. Season, September to May.

Physicians. — Drs. Hicks, Grabham, M. Petta.

Hotels.—New Hotel, St. Clara, Carmo, Edenboro, German Hotel, Victoria.

SWITZERLAND.

In general this is a cold and often wet country, even in summer-time, when people visit it. The elevation of the region accounts for this. Geneva itself, at its entrance, is rarely hot for more than a day or so in summer. In some of the narrow valleys the heat is at times oppressive, but in most of the high regions it is quite cold up to July and August, and in some years even during these months. The elevation of the country is 700 to 15,000 feet. The winters are long and cold, yet in the highest valleys the sun shines so strongly that in mid-winter it is possible to go skating in summer clothing. This makes a favoured region for those who can stand a cold climate, as its bracing air cannot be got elsewhere. Outside of this region, however, Switzerland is mostly a country to visit for pleasure, not for health.

The mineral waters of the country are, however, important, and the Swiss are clever in providing cures of all kinds at their springs. Over four hundred places are mentioned as health resorts; when they do not have mineral waters they give the grape, milk and air cures; and Switzerland has come to be looked upon, not quite justly, as an international sanitarium. The general excellence and fair terms of its hotels are the feature that should be most spoken of, and its beautiful scenery cannot be too much praised.

Even if it be argued that there are spots on the earth that are quite as pretty, still it cannot be said that the same excellent accommodation can be had in so many accessible places of such beauty and magnificence, as those we find in Switzerland.

SULPHUR SPRINGS.

Louèche (Canton Valais).

395 miles from Paris, viâ Lausanne to Louèche station; thence coach in three hours for Louèche-les-Bains; twenty-five hours, eighty-five francs.

Waters.—They are sulphate of lime springs, containing arsenic and iron, some twenty wells in all. The old habit of long immersions is kept up here; people bathe for hours together, in a common bath, with little tables before them for chess, work, &c.

Therapeutics. — Chronic skin diseases, scrofula, rheumatism, gout, uterine complaints.

The baths of Louèche, in German *Leukerbad,* are situated in a small and rather wild and dull-looking valley. The altitude is 4,600 feet, the climate is variable with cold mornings and evenings. From the 15th of June to September is the rather short season. The place is much visited, some 6,000 in summer coming for the waters. It is at the foot of the Gemmi, a high mountain of the Bernese Alps, and excellent excursions can be made from here.

The grape cure is used here at the end of September.

Physicians.—Drs. Brunner, De Werra, De La Harpe.

Hotels.—The Grand Hôtel des Alpes, on an elevation, is the largest house ; France, Union, Bellevue.

BADEN (NEAR ZURICH).

370 miles from Paris, E. of F.R.R., viâ Basel ; fifteen hours, sixty-six francs.

Waters.—These are hot sulphur springs, 120° Fah. It is a weak water of the indifferent class, and depends on its heat for its curative effects.

Therapeutics.—Rheumatism, gout, uterine troubles, syphilis, paralysis.

Baden in Switzerland, Canton Argovia, is on the river Limmat, and is a cheerful resort in a mild climate. Altitude, 1,180 feet. Life is cheap and very quiet here, and the old-fashioned hotels are very quaint. The whey cure is in use. Population, 3,500. The old town is surrounded by walls. The excursions to Zürich, Lucerne, and the Bernese Oberland are near.

Physicians. — Drs. Borsinger, Minnich, Schmidt.

Hotels.—Bahnhof, Linde, Telegraphe.

SCHINZNACH (CANTON ARGOVIA.)

370 miles from Paris, E. of F.R.R., viâ Belfort and Basel, fifteen hours, seventy francs.

Waters.—Hot sulphate of lime springs, 95° Fah. They are exciting to the skin like most such waters. The baths are taken from one to two hours at a time like many others in Switzerland.

Therapeutics.—Skin diseases, lichen, scrofula, catarrhs, lead poisoning.

Schinznach, also called "Habsburg," is at an altitude of 1,100 feet, at the foot of the Wülpelsberg, on the river Aar.   Population, 1,500.   Visitors, 5,000.   The baths are very large, and could hold three persons.   It has a mild climate, healthy and soft ; not much rain. Season, May to September.   The place is most picturesquely situated.   Notice ruins of the old castle of the Habsburgs.*

Physicians.—Drs. Amsler, Hemman and Dr. Tymowski (speaks English).

Hotels.—Établissement, Thermal.

Books.—Dr. Tymowski has a work in English on the waters.

Saxon-les-Bains (Canton Valais).

Waters.—Bromo-iodurated waters, 60° Fah. The milk and grape cures are also given.

Route.—From Martigny over the Simplon. Five miles from Martigny, which see.

---

* *Wildegg* is a strong sulphur spring, only three miles from Schinznach; its waters are given at the last place.   They are cold and said to contain iodine.

Therapeutics.—Syphilis, scrofula, gout.

The waters contain iodine and bromine.

Climate mild and healthy ; good wines and grapes.

Saxon is situated in the fertile valley of the Rhone, and is a well-arranged establishment. Gambling was at one time allowed here, and brought crowds of visitors.   The place is now quiet and suitable for invalids.   The environs are picturesque ; fine excursions.

Physician.—Dr. Dénériaz.

ALKALINE SPRINGS, OR INDIFFERENT WATERS.

RAGATZ-PFÄFFERS (CANTON SAINT-GALL).

445 miles from Paris, E.R.R. viâ Zürich ; seventeen and a half hours, eighty francs.

Waters.—These bicarbonated springs are clear and hot, 96° to 104° Fah., and have no special taste.   They are tonic and digestive. The waters of Pfäffers are brought to Ragatz and used here.   They are said to resemble those of Gastein in Austria.

Therapeutics.—Dyspepsia, gastralgia, nervous diseases, women's complaints, hysteria.

Ragatz-Pfäffers has a population of 2,000; altitude, 1,600 feet. It is situated in a beautiful plain on the River Tameria, and as is often the case in Switzerland, is as much frequented for the scenery as the waters.

Physicians.—Drs. Dormann, Jäger, Kaiser.

Hotels.—Quellenhof, Hof Ragatz, Tameria.

SALINE WATERS.

AIGLE-LES-BAINS.

Aigle, Canton Vaud; Montreux to *Bex;* altitude about 1,400 feet. See Montreux for route and cost. Salt waters and electric baths. There is also milk and whey cure.

Therapeutics.—This place is recommended for a quiet place for treatment of nervous patients, neurasthenia, &c.

Aigle has a fine hotel and large château, with romantic scenery. The Grand Hôtel is on a hill about one and a quarter miles above the village itself, where there are small hotels and pensions.   There is an English Church at the Grand Hôtel, in a separate building. This hotel has extensive grounds, and is suitable for a prolonged stay in summer. Good excursions and hills around, but no special amusements.

Physicians. — Drs. Maudrin and Verey (Swiss).

Grand Hôtel.

IRON WATERS AND SUMMER AND WINTER CLIMATE STATION.

SAINT-MORITZ (ENGADINE VALLEY).

505 miles from Paris, viâ Basel and Coire ; thirty hours, 100 francs.   From London, £7.

Waters.—These are cold iron springs containing carbonic acid gas, but the place is more used as a climatic mountain resort.

Therapeutics. — Anæmia and chlorosis, general debility, chest diseases, uterine and vaginal catarrhs, scrofula, nervous affections, convalescence after all severe diseases.

The village of *Saint-Moritz*, Canton Grisons on the Inn, is the highest in the Engadine, 6,111 feet, and is separated by a distance of a little over a mile from Saint-Moritz-Bad, some 300 feet above. The air here is exceedingly pure ; organic impurities are present in such small quantity that the air is considered aseptic. There are no manufactories to spoil the atmosphere which is quite dry, first from the altitude and the nature of the climate, and also from the fact that Saint-Moritz has the smallest rainfall in Switzerland. The air too is thin, and has peculiar qualities owing to the near glaciers and the presence of ozone. In winter it is said that delicate persons can sit out in the open air for a greater number of hours and days than in summer. It is, of course, from the nature of its bright, stimulating and very cold air, not suitable to persons who have poor circulation, such as old people and also those subject to hæmorrhages, plethora, &c.

30,000 visitors ; boating and fishing, skating in winter. The rarefied cold-air cure is now in great repute. In fine weather the place is delightful, and the climate exhilarating ; but, as above stated, it must not be sought by those who feel cold and do not care for sharp, bracing air. Snow falls but rarely in summer ; in winter it lies close upon six months, from November to March. Take warm clothing here even in summer.

Physicians. — Drs. Holland, St. Clair Thompson (English).

American Dentist.—H. L. Schaffner.

Hotels.—Curhaus, Victoria, Du Lac, Engadiner Hof. Write beforehand in summer for rooms.

Books.—See Dr. Holland's work on Saint-Moritz, in English.

TARASP (ENGADINE).

531 miles from Paris, viâ Basel to Ponte, whence diligence in four hours, twenty-four hours, eighty-eight francs.

Waters.—Cold soda and iron springs, not very strong. Considered diuretic and laxative in large doses.

Therapeutics.—Dyspepsia, liver diseases, anæmia. Kidney and bladder troubles are made a speciality.   There are both alkaline and iron springs ; twenty-three wells in all.

The baths of Tarasp, called *Tarasp-Schuls*, are situated in the Canton of Grisons, about 4,000 feet above sea-level.   This little place is one of the most picturesque of Switzerland. It is renowned for the beauty of its excursions. Vulpera is a suburb formed of hotels ; thence the gorge of Clemgia and Inn leads to Schuls. The climate is rather brisk with sudden changes, and a dry, tonic air that suits robust people.   Season, from the 15th of June to the 30th of September.   Tarasp combines iron, alkaline, purgative waters, with the high mountain-air cure.   Scarcely another station in Europe unites so many important qualities.

Physicians.—Drs. Pernisch, Killias.

Hotels.—Belvedere, Poste, Helvetia, Kur-haus.

———

COLD, DRY, WINTER CLIMATIC STATIONS.

DAVOS-PLATZ (GRISONS).

Route.—It is fifteen miles from Coire station, but the railroad is now finished to

Landquart station near by. From London,
£6 14s. 9d.

Davos-Platz is one of the highest inhabited
places in Europe ; it is about a mile above
sea-level. Twenty-seven years ago two
German consumptives passed a winter here,
and they still survive, living testimonies of
the value of this form of climatic treatment.
At present more than 1,500 patients pass the
winter at Davos, and a smaller number at other
high mountain stations, such as the *Maloya,
Wiesen, Campher*, and *Saint-Moritz*. It is
very curious that in midwinter, when the
snow lies dry and powdery on the ground
the radiating solar thermometer marks 110° F.
At the same time the temperature of the air
in the shade is 10° below freezing-point ;
yet, notwithstanding this, a person can sit out
in the air without an overcoat, and barely
support the heat of the sun. The pure, clear,
thin, dry, cold air facilitates radiation, and
permits the transmission of the sun's rays,
and the white snow reflects the heat. It is
owing to this dryness and stillness of the
atmosphere that patients can thus enjoy the

sun's heat, and not be bothered with the coldness of the air. In December, January and February cloudless days are frequent.

The important question is—what classes of cases can be sent with advantage to this dry, cold, stimulating climate? The vital forces of the patients sent here must be strong, so that they can re-act under the stimulation. People who like cold weather and feel well under its influence improve here as a rule. Toboganning, sledging and skating attract many here.

Therapeutics. — Neurasthenia, anæmia, convalesence, dyspepsia and certain forms of phthisis. Here the general habit and temperament of the patient are of such vast importance that no patient should be sent to these climates except by a physician who understands not only the climate but the constitution of the patient. Nervous asthma does well here, but not when dependent upon emphysema.

The town is now well-drained, and lighted with electricity.

20

Physicians.—Dr. W. K. Huggard (English), Dr. Tucker-Wise, Dr. Spengler (Swiss).

Hotels.—Victoria, Angleterre, Belvedere, Schweizer Hof.

SWISS SUMMER STATIONS.

GENEVA.

Eleven hours from Paris by P.L.M.R.R., seventy francs, or fifty second class. The evening express carries second class. From London, £6 2s.

Therapeutics.—This city is not a health resort, but it is the gateway to Switzerland, and deserves mention for several reasons. The annual death rate is only fifteen, one of the lowest in Europe. The sewerage system is admirably managed. The drains empty into two large collecting channels, one on each side of the River Rhone, which pours from the lake. The current is very swift here, and every impurity is rapidly carried far below the city, and destroyed by the force of the current and the richness of the water in oxygen. The drinking water is drawn from the lake above all this, and is very pure. This accounts for the place being healthy, notwithstanding the rather severe climate. In summer it is dusty and dull; foreigners only pass through the city, resting for a day or two at most. It is often very windy.

Geneva has an altitude of 1,227 feet, and its meteorological variations are those of the Alpine regions in general. The average winter temperature is 35° Fah., summer 76° Fah. There are hardly any amusements in summer. In winter there are good performances in a very pretty theatre on the model of the Grand Opera in Paris.

Physicians.—Drs. Cordés, M.R.C.P., and Vulliet; they speak English.

American Dentist.—Hurlburt.

American Church.—The Rev. Adamson.

Hotels.—National, De La Paix, Russie, Des Bergues, La Genève, Victoria, Bellevue. All good and reasonable.

Books.—The town publishes a good guide in English for one franc.

MONTREUX.

Route by R.R. from Geneva, but it is better to take the steamer up the lake in six hours. From London, £6 5s. 3d. Montreux really includes several stations which are close to it. *Clarens*, *Vernex-Montreux*, *Territet-Glion*, and *Veytaux*. These places have grown together, and form one whole under the district name of Montreux. This is certainly the prettiest part of Lake Leman or Geneva. Well-sheltered, it is a favourite resort for autumn and spring, and many persons make it a winter residence. It is a climatic and intermediate station with a grape cure in the fall. The winter climate is crisp and bright, and though the rainfall is heavy, fifty inches, there are many clear days. The best season is autumn. This north-eastern shore of the lake, as we have said, is the grandest and most picturesque part. The place is very popular with the English, and its climate is certainly heaven in comparison with their own. It is *not* a warm winter climate as some make the mistake of describing it.

The winter temperature gives a mean of 36" Fah.

Glion is a mountain station over Montreux that has a switchback railway connecting it with the last town. It is readily accessible. The hotels are very comfortable here, as they are at *Vevey* lower down the lake, and are connected by electric tramway with Montreux. The views are magnificent. Milk and whey cure.

Physician.—Dr. Stuart Tidey, M.R.C.P. London.

Hotels. — Roy, Beau Rivage, National, Cygne.

LUCERNE.

E. of F.R.R. viâ Basel, nineteen hours from Paris, seventy francs. From London, £5 6s. 9d.

Lucerne is very much visited but is hardly a health resort. It rains a great deal in the place, but the wonderful beauty of the lake and environs attracts a number of visitors. The Rigi is the incomparable attraction. It has no special cures.

Physician.—Dr. A. Hill Hassall (English).
Hotels. — Schweitzerhof, Beau Rivage. Balance, Angleterre.

PHYSICIANS' OR MEDICAL DIRECTORY OF EUROPE.

THE list is made by countries, and includes the names, as far as possible, of physicians who speak English, or those who are themselves English or American. The German doctors mostly speak English fairly well. The French rarely speak any language but their own. A. is for American, E. for English, F. for French, G. for German.

Many persons, on arriving in a new town, are in the habit of asking almost any stranger to recommend them a physician. But we cannot too strongly advise English and American travellers to be chary of patronising either professional or commercial people, who are recommended by servants, couriers, concierges, hotel agents, &c., without having first inquired of their consul or clergyman, or of some 'friend, as to the standing of the persons recommended.

It would be well for persons visiting Europe to obtain the addresses of competent professional men before leaving home, because local advice is not always disinterested, and the poor stranger may be confided to the tender mercies of an advertising quack. It not unfrequently happens that interested parties plot together, as a matter of personal gain, without any regard whatever for the well-being of those whom they advise.

AUSTRIA-HUNGARY.

Abbazia.—Dr. von Hausen.

Arco. — Drs. Althammer, Schreiber, Schilder.

Baden.—Drs. Barth, Schwartz.

Buda-Pest or Ofen.—Drs. von Heinrich, Verzar.

Carlsbad.—Drs. Ables, Gans, Grünberger, Hoffmeister, Kraus, London, Neubauer, Mayer, Rosenzweig.

Franzensbad. — Drs. Egger, Klein, Loimann, Sommer, Steinschneider.

Gastein.—Drs. Bunzel, Proell, Schneider.

Ischl.—Drs. Kahn, Fürstenberg, Steiger.

Innsbruck.—Drs. Ehrendorfer, Glatz, Rokitansky.

Levico.—Drs. Arenini, Pacher, Sartou.

Marienbad.—Drs. David Lucker, Lucca, Schindler, Barney.

Méran.—Braitenberg, Fischer, Hirschfeld, Huber, Kittel, Kuhn, Ludernur, Proell, Messing, Schreiber, Veninger.

Teplitz.—Drs. Baumeister, Hirsch, Kraus, Langstein, Lieblein, Mandel, Stein.

Voslau.—Drs. Krische, Veninger.

Vienna.—Professor Billroth, Kolingasse 6; Professor Albert, Maximilian-Platz 7; von Mosetig, Fleischmarkt 1; Hofmohl, Heffer Strasse 9; and von Dittel, Aller Strasse 4; are surgeons.

Physicians.—Professor Nothnagel, Rathhaus Gasse 13; Professor Oser, Reichraths Gasse 25; Dr. Drasche, Wollzeile 4; and Dr. Augustus R. Kosack (speaks English), Nibelungen Gasse 7.

Skin Diseases.—Professor Neumann,

Rotherthurm Strasse 29; Professor Kaposi, Alser Strasse 28; Dr. Hebra, Kohlmarkt 7.

Eye Diseases.—Professor Fuchs, Oppolzer Gasse 9; Professor Stellwag, Schottenhof 12.

Ear Diseases.—Professor Politzer, Gonzs Gasse 19; Dr. Gruber, Freitung 7; Dr. Bing, Grünanger Gasse 12.

Women's Diseases.—Professor Chrobak, Brauner Strasse 9; Professor Braun, Seiler Strasse 1; Professor Rokitansky, Kärntne Ring 2.

Children's Diseases.—Professor Wiederhofer, Planken Gasse 3; Dr. Kassowitz, Freichlanberg 9; Dr. Monti, Rosen Gasse 8.

Nervous Complaints.—Professor Meyners, Pelikan Gasse 14; Benedict, Franziskaner Platz 5.

Throat Diseases.—Professor Schrotter, Mariannen Gasse 3; Professor Chiari, Bellaria Strasse 12.

Hydropathy.—Professor Winternitz, Helferstorfer Gasse 9.

Dentists.—Dr. Scheff, Hoher Markt 4; Dr. Pichler, Stefans Platz 6.

BELGIUM AND HOLLAND.

Ostende.—Drs. Gerard, Janssen, Van Dyl.
Spa.—Drs. Cafferata (E.), Damseau (F.).
Scheveningen.—Drs. Fracken, Mess.

FRANCE.

Aix-les-Bains.—(F.) Drs. Bertier, Blanc, Brachet, Coze, Cazalis, M'Roé, Forestier, Francon, Gaston, Guilland, Legrand, Macé, Monard, Petit and Vidal ; (E.) Dr. Stanley-Rendall ; (A.) Thomas Linn, M.D.
Allevard.—Drs. Isoard ; Niepce.
Ajaccio.—Dr. Malgréni.
Amphion.—Dr. Dumur.
Algiers.—(E.) Dr. Thompson ; (A.) Dr. Pepper.
Arcachon. — Drs. Festal, Hameau, Lalesque.
Bagnères de Bigorre. — Drs. Bagnell, Middleton (E.)
Barèges.—Dr. Grilmaud.
Bourboule (La).—Drs. Gilchrist (E.), Bertrand, Nicolas, Veyrières (F.).
Beaulieu.—

Boulogne-sur-Mer.—Drs. Bourgain, Gros, Potin.

Biarritz.—Drs. Malpas, MacKew (E.), Adéma (F.).

Brides.—Drs. Delastre, Desprez, Phillabert.

Cannes.—Drs. Bright, Blanc, Frank, Duke (E.), Agnes McLaren, Dr. De Valcourt, Daremberg.

Cauterets.—Drs. Dehourcau, Bordenave, Flurin.

Challes.—Drs. Royer, Raugé.

Châtel-Guyon.—Dr. Baraduc.

Contrexéville. — Drs. Debout, Estrées, Boursier, Graux.

Dax.—Drs. Barthe de Sandfort, Lerema.

Dieppe.—Drs. Caron, De la Rue, Parel.

Eaux Bonnes.—Drs. Cazaux, Cazenave de la Roche.

Évian.—Drs. Roques, Mellion, Taberlet.

Enghien.—Drs. Japhet, Weill.

Forges.—Drs. Cavé, Mathon.

Grasse.—Drs. Chabert, Laugier.

Hyères.—Drs. Biden, Cormack (E.); Bourgarel (F.).

Luchon.—Drs. Ferras, Fontan de Laverenne, Kühnemann.

Mentone or Menton. — Drs. Fitzhenry, Siordet, Marriott, and Stanley-Rendall (E.); Dr. Roques (F.).

Monte Carlo (Monaco).—Drs. Fagge, Fitz-gerald, Hutchinson, Mitchell, Pickering (all E.).

Montmirail.—Dr. Millet.

Mont-Dore.—Drs. Chabory, Edmond, Joel, Cazalis, Nicholas.

Néris.—Dr. Ranze, Grandmaison.

Nice. — Drs. Ashmore-Noakes, Brandt, Gilchrist (E.) and Thomas Linn, M.D. (American), Quai Masséna 16, and W. A. Sturge.

Pierrefonds.—Drs. Janvier, Bourgarel.

Pougues.—Drs. Bovet, Janicot.

Plombières.—Drs. Bottentuit, Malebran, Lietard.

Pau.—Drs. Bagnall, Hunt, Clay (E.).

PARIS.

(A.) Drs. Austin, 29, Rue Cambon; Boyland, 73, Avenue d'Antin; Clarke, 17, Rue de Suresne; Dunn, Rue Pyramides 15; Good, Ave. du Bois de Boulogne 23; Bull (oculist), 4, Rue de la Paix ; Dr. Warren Bey, of Baltimore, 15, Rue Caumartin ; (E.) Drs. Barnard, 342, Rue Saint-Honoré ; Chapman, Ave. de l'Opera ; Dupuy, Ave. Montaigne 53 ; Dr. Hon. Alan Herbert, Rue Duphot 18 ; O. Jennings, Rue Marbeuf 33 ; Loughnan, 38, Rue de Berri ; Prendergast, Rue de Antin 1 ; MacGavin, Rue de Roule 4.

(F.) *Surgeons.*—Prof. Lannelogne, Rue François Ire 3 ; Prof. Le Fort, Rue de la Victoire 96 ; Dr. Labbé Bould, Ave. Haussman 117 ; Dr. Péan, Boul. Malesherbes 24.

Genito-Urinary.—Professor Guyon, Rue Roquepine 11 ; Dr. Fort, Rue François Ire 31.

Physicians.—Professor Germain Sée, Ave. Montaigne 53 ; Professor Potain, Boul. Saint-Germain 256 ; Professor Dieulafoy, Ave. Montaigne 38 ; Professor Bouchard, Rue de Rivoli 174 ; Professor Peter, Rue de Hambourg 20 ; Dr. Henri Huchard, Ave. Champs Élysées 67.

Nervous Diseases. — Professor Charcot, Boul. Saint-Germain 217.

Women's Diseases. — Professor Tarnier,

Rue Duphot 17 ; Dr. Budin, Boul. Saint-Germain 238.

Medico-Legal and Hygiene. — Professor Brouardel, Boul. Saint-Germain 124 ; Professor Proust, Boul. Malesherbes 9.

Eye Diseases.—Professor Panas, Rue de Général Foy 17 ; Dr. Galesowski, Boul. Haussman 103 ; Dr. Landolt, Rue Vonney 2 ; Dr. Bull, Rue de la Paix 4.

Ears.—Dr. Loewenberg, Rue Auber 15.

Throat.—Dr. Fauvel, Ave. de l'Opéra 13 ; Dr. Gougenheim, Boul. Haussman 73.

Children's Diseases.—Professors Gracher, Rue Beaufon 36 ; Dr. Hutenel, Rue de la Boétie 13 ; Dr. Legroux, Rue de Rivoli 178.

Syphilis. — Professor Fournier, Rue Volney 1 ; Dr. Mauriac, Rue Grétry 2.

Skin Diseases. — Dr. Besnier, Rue de Mathurins 37 ; Dr. Vidal, Rue d'Anjou 65 ; Dr. Quinquand, Rue de l'Odéon 5.

Electricity.—Dr. Apostoli, Rue Molière 5 ; Dr. Good, Ave. Bois de Boulogne 23.

Dentists.—Dr. Barclay, Rue de la Paix 5 ; Dr. Evans (Thos.), Rue de la Paix 15 ; Dr.

Evans (John), Ave. de l'Opéra 15 ; Mr. Moore, Ave. d' l'Opéra 36.

Royat.—Drs. Brandt (E.) ; Petit (speaks E.) ; Fredet (F.).

Salins.—Drs. Guyenot, Bourny.

Salies de Béarn. — Drs. Musgrave Clay (E.) ; Dupuyron (F.).

Saint-Malo.—Drs. Ferrand, Noury.

Saint Jean de Luz.—Dr. Goyénèche.

Saint-Honore.—Drs. Collin, Odin.

Saint Sauveur.—Drs. Blondin, Gaulet, Lafont.

Trouville.—Drs. Legoupil, Leneven.

Vichy.—Drs. Cormack (E.), Velleman (F.)

Vittel.—Drs. Bouloumié, Rodet.

Uriage.—Drs. Doyon, Teulon-Valio.

Aix-la-Chapelle.—Drs. Brandis, Schuster, Mayer, Lersch, Schumacher.

Baden-Baden.—Drs. Heiligenthal, Berton, Offenger, Baumgärtner.

Cuxhaven.—Dr. Halssen.

Ems.—Drs. Döring, Flattmann, Geisse, Orth, Reuter, Vogler.

Falkenstein.—Dr. Dettweiler.

Görbersdorf.—Dr. Brehmer.

Homburg.—Drs. Schetelig, Deetz, Weber, Hoeber.

Kissingen.—Drs. Dietz, Stohr.

Kreuznach.—Drs. Engelmann, Jung, Strahl, Wolff, Lier, Weber.

Nauheim.—Drs. Bode, Friedländer, Müller, Schott.

Neuenahr.—Drs. Schmitz, Teschemacher, Unschuld.

Pyrmont. — Drs. Schücking, Köhler, Lynker, Seebohm.

Schwalbach.—Drs. Boehm, Gubert, Freckhofer.

Schlangenbad. — Drs. Baumann, Wolff, Grossmann.

ˉ*Soden.*—Drs. Thilenius, Haupt, ˉHughes, Stoltzing, Fresenius.

Wiesbaden. — Drs. Pagensticker, Ricker, Metzger, Pfeiffer, Ziemssen.

BERLIN.

Surgeons. — Professors von Bergmann, Alexander Strasse 1 ; Dr. Hahn, Charlotten Strasse 59.

Physicians.--Professors Leyden, Thiergarten Strasse 14 ; Dr. Oppert (M.R.C.P.London) Ring Strasse 57 ; Friedenau.

Eye Diseases. — Dr. Fröhlich, Oranien Strasse 47 ; Dr. Schweiger, Roon Strasse 6.

Ear Diseases. — Dr. Dennert, Alexander Strasse 44 ; Dr. Lucae, Voss Strasse 32.

Women's Diseases.—Dr. Guserow, Roon Strasse 4 ; Dr. Martin.

Nervous Diseases. — Dr. Eulenberg, Litzow Strasse 60 ; Dr. Jastrowitz, Louisen Strasse 29.

Children's Diseases.—Dr. Baginski, Potsdamer Strasse 5 ; Dr. Schutte, Anhalt Strasse 13.

Throat Diseases.—Dr. Fränkel, Neuesbad Strasse 12 ; Dr. Fräntzel, Karlsbad Strasse 3 ; Dr. Schotz, Potsdamer Strasse 20.

Dresden.—(A.) Dr. A. T. Watson, 22 Racknitz Strasse ; (E.) Dr. Pierson.

Frankfort-am-Main.—Dr. AdamsWalther.

GREAT BRITAIN.

Bath.—Drs. Brabazon, Budd, Spender, Freeman.

Buxton. — Drs. Bennett, Flint, Turner, Robertson.

Cheltenham.—Drs. Abercrombie, Bennett, Cottle, Roch.

Clifton.—Dr. E. Williams.

Harrogate. — Drs. Oliver, Helmsley-Walker, Johnson-Lavis, Ward.

Llandrindod.—Dr. Davies.

Leamington. — Drs. Wilmot, Holmer, Thursfield.

Matlock.—Drs. Hunter, Whitby.

Moffatt.—Dr. D'Otley Grange.

Tunbridge Wells.—Drs. Rix, Rankin.

Strathpeffer. — Drs. Manson, Middleton, Fox.

Woodhall Spa.—Dr. E. Williams.

LONDON.

Surgeons. — Professor Holmes, 18, Great Cumberland Place; Sir J. Paget, 1, Harewood Place; Mr. Victor Horsley, 80, Park Street, Grosvenor Square; Mr. Bryant, 65, Grosvenor Street; Mr. Nunn, 8, Stratford Place; Sir J. Lister, 12, Park Crescent, Portland Place.

Physicians. — Sir R. Quain, 67, Harley Street; Dr. Broadbent, 34, Seymour Street; Dr. Bristowe, 13, Old Burlington Street; Dr. M. Bruce, 70, Harley Street; Dr. Brunton, 10, Stratford Place; Dr. F. Roberts, 102, Harley Street; Sir A. Clark, 16, Cavendish Square; Dr. T. D. Acland, 7, Brook Street; Sir Dyce Duckworth, 11, Grafton Street; Dr. B. Howard, 8, Hanover Square; Dr. McNeill Whistler, 28, Wimpole Street; Dr. Sansom, 84, Harley Street.

Chest Diseases. —Dr. Douglas Powell, 62, Wimpole Street; Dr. Theo. Williams, 2, Upper Brook Street; Dr. Kingston Fowler, 35, Clarges Street.

Nose Diseases. —Dr. Woakes, 78, Harley Street; Dr. Semon, 39, Wimpole Street.

Heart. —Dr. A. E. Sansom, 84, Harley Street.

Nervous Diseases. —Dr. Hughlings Jackson, 3, Manchester Square; Dr. Gowers, 50, Queen Anne Street; Dr. S. Wilks, 72, Grosvenor Street.

Children's Diseases. — Dr. Cheadle, 18,

Portman Street; Dr. Eustace Smith, 5, George Street, Hanover Square.

Eye Diseases.—Dr. Nettleship, 5, Wimpole Street; Mr. Critchett, 21, Harley Street; Mr. H. E. Juler, 77, Wimpole Street; Dr. McHardy, 5, Saville Row.

Ear Diseases.—Dr. Pritchard, 3, George Street, Hanover Square; Sir William Dalby, 18, Saville Row.

Women's Diseases.—Sir Spencer Wells, 3, Upper Grosvenor Street; Dr. Barnes, 15, Harley Street; Dr. Braxton Hicks, 24, George Street, Hanover Square.

Skin Diseases.—Mr. Jonathan Hutchinson, 15, Cavendish Square; Dr. E. Thin, 22, Queen Anne Street: Dr. J. J. Pringle, 35, Bruton Street.

Bladder Diseases.—Sir H. Thompson, 35, Wimpole Street; Mr. H. Fenwick, 5, Old Burlington Street.

Health Resorts.—Dr. H. Weber, 10, Grosvenor Street; Dr. Yeo, 44, Hertford Street, Mayfair.

ITALY.

Acqui.—Dr. Dom.

Alassio.—Dr. Dickinson (E.).

Bordighera.—Dr. Goodchild (E.).

Genoa.—Dr. Breiting.

Nervi.—Dr. Schetelig.

Monte Cateni.—Dr. Casciani.

Lucca.—Drs. Gason (E.); Georgi.

La Poretta.—Dr. Castelli.

San Remo.—Drs. Freeman, Hassell, Shuttleworth (E).

Florence.—(A.) Dr. Baldwin; (E.) Drs. Coldstream, St. Clair-Thompson, Wilson.

Rome.—Dr. Gason, F. C. Martley, Thompson, Charles, Spurway, Young (E.).

Naples.—Drs. Gairdner, Barrenger, Johnson-Lavis.

SPAIN.

Archena.—Drs. Zavala, Velasco.

Carratraca.—Drs. Salgado, T. Gunelem.

Ledesma.—Drs. Garcia, Lopez.

Saint-Sebastian.—Dr. W. J. Smith (E.).

Malaga.—Dr. Bundsen.

Madeira.—Drs. Hicks, Grabham, Petta.

22

SWITZERLAND.

Baden. — Drs. Borsenger, Minnich, Schmidt.

Davos-Platz.—Drs. Huggard, Tucker, Wise (E.), Spengler (S.).

Geneva.—Drs. Cordes, Vulliet.

Louèche.—Drs. Bremer, De Werra, De la Harpe.

Montreux.—Dr. Stuart Tidey (E.).

Ragatz.—Drs. Dorman, Jäger, Kaiser.

Saxon.—Dr. Démériez.

Schinznach.—Drs. Amsler, Tymoski.

Saint-Moritz.—Drs. Holland, St. Clair-Thompson.

Tarasp.—Drs. Perrish, Killias.

GENERAL ALPHABETICAL INDEX.